Rescuing Madison

by
Terry Brody

Acknowledgements

This book is for the two girls that put a smile on my face every day, my wife Christine & my daughter Riley.

Special thanks to Elizabeth Robertson Laytin, Amanda McLoughlin, John Brody and book cover designer, Randy Rosand.

Check out rescuingmadison.com for giveaways, to blog, or for info on Terry Brody's next book, "Adrian of Death."
To share feedback on the book with the author, email him at terrybrody@gmail.com.

1

I . . .Don't

Country music plays softly inside the patrol car. Nine-year-old Madison Park rides alongside her dad, Sheriff Park. They sing along to the song on a beautiful, autumn day in the country. Sheriff Park has quite the voice and the two of them together could be a successful father/daughter act. But Madison's father is a simple, small town man, although, nobody would argue that he is the biggest fish in the small town of Wynona, Oklahoma.

Huge trees with the most beautiful, colored leaves line the streets as the sheriff's cruiser slowly navigates its way through town. The locals, one by one, wave to their lone lawman as the cruiser passes.

The sheriff's car pulls into a small parking lot behind a row of stores and parks. He lowers the radio and leaves the car running. Before he gets out he boasts to his young daughter, "I'm going to make your mom the best meal she's ever had."

"You're so romantic," young Madison says, as she looks up at her dad.

Her father gets out of the car and heads into the liquor store to pick out the perfect bottle of wine to compliment the perfect meal. For a small town liquor store, there's a large selection of wines — mostly from California. The owner Gabe has always been a wine lover. Gabe is a pleasant, old man in his late seventies that should have retired fifteen years ago.

Sheriff Park enters and Gabe puts his newspaper down as they greet each other. "How's business?" Sheriff Park asks.

Gabe's response is more fateful than one could ever imagine. "Uneventful," Gabe says, and gets back to his newspaper.

Sheriff Park scans the assortment of wines.

Out in front of the store a car pulls up. A man dressed in a long coat gets out of the passenger side and looks to his left, then his right. He enters the store, approaches Gabe at the counter and — from underneath the coat — pulls a shotgun. The man puts the huge gun to Gabe's face and demands money. The sheriff is only about ten feet away but the man is so focused on getting the cash he doesn't see him. Gabe is terrified as he instinctively turns his head toward Sheriff Park as if to ask his advice on the situation.

Sheriff Park has to act fast.

The armed robber follows Gabe's eyes until his own are staring into those of Sheriff Park. Surprise. The sheriff draws his gun faster than Billy the Kid and orders the robber to drop his weapon. In a split second it becomes obvious the man isn't backing down. The two men fire simultaneously.

In the rear parking lot Madison sings along with the country song when gunshots ring out. She pops up, startled.

***

The wheels of Madison Park's private jet touch the ground making a loud noise. Madison, now twenty-one awakens and nearly jumps out of her seat. She peers out the window, only to see thousands of fans surrounding the airport terminal. Not to mention, the scores of media people. She can't help but think, "What good is a private jet if I have to go through the airport terminal?" She closes her eyes and tries to get another short nap before she has to face her public.

***

Love is in the air as a fire truck speeds along a New York City street. Frank, a huge, muscular African-American firefighter drives because he has the most time in the fire company. He's the "senior man." Our fearless leader, Captain Jack – handle-bar mustache and all – sits in the passenger seat. Sirens blare and

3

lights flash as my buddy John is about to do something I am very much against – at his age anyway. He's only twenty-three. I'm Billy; I'm a little older and a lot wiser than my firefighting counterpart so I feel compelled to talk some sense into him.

"The rest of your life is a mighty long time," I tell him.

"I sure hope so," John replies with a raise of his eyebrows.

"You don't have to do this. Never underestimate what you're up against. If you're not ready, you're gonna get burned."

"Don't worry about me, I rely on my instinct," John confidently shoots back, as he gets his firefighting gear on.

Not far away, Melissa, an aspiring actress in her early twenties, with raven-like, straight, black hair and big, teddy bear, brown eyes folds clothes in her cramped apartment. She has sharp, facial features and a brash, Brooklyn attitude. The stereo is blasting one of Madison Park's recent hits and Melissa's in a zone. She hears only the music and sees only the pile of laundry when suddenly lights flash outside her window. She has no idea that black smoke is billowing from the roof.

Outside, the fire truck screeches to a halt. Frank gets out and sets up the truck for fire duty. A crowd gathers as John jumps in the truck's bucket.

"You don't have to do this," I shout, giving it one more shot.

"I want to do this," John says.

4

John doesn't seem to be nervous as the bucket rises high in the air. When it reaches the window John sticks his tool underneath and pries it open. In a panic inside the apartment, Melissa runs over to John at the window and says, "Oh my God, what's happening, what's going on?"

In his manliest voice, John orders her out of the window and into the bucket. She instinctively goes.

"Where's the fire?" She asks, panicked. "What's going on, John?"

John puts his arms on Melissa's shoulders in an attempt to calm her, "Melissa, I'm here to rescue you."

Could he be any cornier?

John kneels as the thick black smoke continues to push from the chimney – as it should. There's no fire. The crowd on the street gasps when John pulls a small velvet box from his pocket.

Now it's Melissa that gasps, "Oh my God."

I feel like vomiting at this point.

But it's apparent John can't hold in his excitement as he cracks a soft smile, holds the box with the sparkling 'bling' and asks, "Melissa, will you marry me?"

Melissa, stunned, is silent. She doesn't say a word. The silence is excruciating for John. Hell, it's hard for me – John's my friend. I may bust his balls but I don't want to see him humiliated in public.

He tries to pry an answer from her lips, "Well, will you be my wife?"

At that awkward moment, John peers in the

window and sees folded clothing in a suitcase, "Are you going somewhere?"

"Chicago, to see my grandmother," Melissa says. "And, I got a part in a play."

"In Chicago? This is New York; you can't get a part in a play in New York?"

"We were supposed to have dinner and talk tonight," Melissa says.

"We were supposed to have dinner and celebrate tonight!"

"You know I'm not happy," she says.

"Actually, I don't."

"I want bigger things for myself, I have big dreams. I want more out of life."

"I get it; you want more than what I can give you."

Suddenly Captain Jack's voice crackles over our handie-talkies, "Romeo, we got a call, we gotta go."

"I'm sorry, John," she says.

2

Did You Say Pianist Or. . .

Total bummer, I know. Let's fast forward to where things get even juicier. I'll introduce myself in a moment. First, let's set up the crazy scene. A tall, well built, man that looks like he should be a professional wrestler waits alongside a white, stretch limousine as a flock of papparazzi emerge from the airport terminal. They move in one big, flashing wave. In the center of the mass is a young blonde wearing sunglasses even though it's a cloudy, autumn day. Madison Park is not just beautiful; she's got more talent than every American Idol winner combined. Her voice is strong and her range is long. That girl can sing in her sleep. She was born with raw talent.

In fact it was her mother that first heard her sing. When Maddy was just nine-years-old, she was taking a shower and singing her little heart out – The Spice Girls, "Wannabe." The bathroom door flew open, her mother ripped aside the shower curtain and made the decision right then and there that she was going to dedicate her life to her young daughter's

7

talent.

Speaking of her mother – Angie Park is everything a mother shouldn't be. But I won't bore you with details of neglect. The bottom line is that she has become Madison's manager and agent, and in the process has lost the role of mother. A brilliantly, talented, motherless child is Madison Park.

As we get into the limo, this is where I come into the picture, I'm Quentin. If it weren't for me, Maddy's hair would be stringy, her makeup would make her look like a "ho" and her outfits would be "retro" without being "retro." She'd look like a skank right outta the movie Footloose. (Okay, I exaggerate. You'll get used to that).

Maddy is gorgeous and she has exquisite taste in everything although she needed a little help in the "What is a sexy man?" category. But we'll get to that. I would do anything and everything for Maddy and, come to think of it, I do – including removing the yellow skittles from her candy dish. She hates yellow. I think it's summery but what-ev. I've known her since she was a young girl. We were best friends and I helped Angie make her a star from the beginning. Since then my responsibilities have increased immensely. I like to think of myself as her "life coach."

8

Sometimes the stress of it all is just too much. I don't know how I do it.

We finally reach the limousine and get in but not before Madison turns, removes her sunglasses and gives the photographers their chance to get a shot of a smiling teen idol – even if the smile is fake.

Inside the limousine, Madison is silent as she gazes out the window at autumn in New York. You would think she was Socrates the way she contemplates. But Maddy isn't thinking about the current state of the Middle East, she's just lonely. Even pop stars get lonely, maybe more so than the rest of us. Think about it, her whole life is work. Sure it's fun but it's exhausting. And if your boyfriend forgot your twenty-first birthday, you'd be quiet too. Although, that was four months ago – you would think she'd have gotten over it by now.

On top of the unreliable, downright delinquent, boyfriend this is a bad time of year for her. It was this week, twelve years ago that her dad died. Nobody brought the girl to life like that man did. Maddy's spirit died along with him. Since then it's like she's just going through the motions. She's like a superstar, celebrity "zombie." I've tried and tried and will never stop trying but since he died nobody has been able to bring that spirit back.

Angie pulls a cigarette from her tin box.

That'll break the silence.

Madison shoots Angie a look and sternly says, "Don't even think about it."

Like I said, there goes the silence.

"I wasn't going to light it," Angie insists.

"Where are we?" Maddy asks.

"New York, honey," Angie replies. "Don't you recognize the big buildings? You love New York."

"I do? What's the difference between New York and every other city? All I get to see is the inside of the hotel; then it's off to the next city. I'd rather be back home in Oklahoma."

I really need to cheer this girl up. And I know just how to do it. "How about a Big Mac?"

Madison peers at me, pretending she's not excited and says, "Make it two and supersize 'em."

"New York has some of the best restaurants in the world. Can't you wait?" Angie asks.

"I want McDonald's," Madison insists.

"How do you eat two Big Mac's?" I ask her. "And where does it go? I am so jealous. I eat a jelly bean and it sticks to my ass."

A few minutes later, the limo pulls into the

drive thru at Micky-D's and Madison gets her food. I swear the girl is gonna turn into a Big Mac.

She's happy now. But the burger can only stave off the loneliness for so long.

***

Back at the firehouse, John and I change for work in the locker room. Like me, John is in great shape. We both just finished a leg workout in the firehouse gym. You can't have wimpy legs as a New York City firefighter. We firemen don't take elevators and New York has some of the biggest buildings in the world. John opens his locker to reveal one single, solitary picture of his ex-girlfriend, Melissa on the inside of his locker door. It's sad, really – but I can help.

"What are you doing Thursday night, John?"

"I'm going to a concert."

"What concert?"

"Jim Brickman," John says, knowing I have no idea who the hell Jim Brickman is.

"Jim who?"

"He's a Jazz pianist."

"He's a penis?" I quizzically ask.

"You're a penis."

"I have a nice penis,"

"Congratulations."

"Why don't you skip the "bore-fest" and come out with me and two hot chicks."

"No thanks."

"Come on." I can't believe I have to beg him. "Do

you remember the school teacher chick that stopped in the firehouse for directions the other day?"

"No."

"She has a friend and women stick together," I say, ignoring him. "So, I don't get her unless her friend gets you."

"I don't think so."

"Please, help me out here."

"Another time," he says.

"You're killing me." I'm pissed so I point to the photograph of Melissa on his locker and say, "It's about time you take that down. It's been six months."

He peers at my beautifully decorated locker and says with biting sarcasm, "Photos of naked porn stars covering every inch of your locker door is much healthier."

"It's a collage – it's art."

"Whatever." John takes his folded work duty shirt from his locker and immediately realizes there's something wrong. He shows me the shirt.

"This is my only clean shirt."

"So?" I respond, playing dumb.

John drops the shirt and it makes a loud thud when it hits the floor. It's frozen.

"I hate when that happens." I smile. "It must be cold in your locker."

"I'll get you for this."

"Why do you assume it's me?"

He reminds me, "Let's see: the cookies in my boots, the hot sauce in my orange juice, and the crickets

12

in the bunk room."

"I have no knowledge of any of those particular events."

"You dropped a bucket of water on me from the roof on my first day here. You soaked my forty dollar Junior's Famous, Brooklyn cheesecake. I was soaking wet when I met Captain Jack."

"You can't prove any of that was me."

"You put my locker on the roof," he says.

"You got changed on the roof for a week before the neighbors complained. I can't understand why they would whine. Seeing a specimen like you in your Calvin Klein's should be a wonderful, rare treat for those deprived souls."

John taps his shirt against his locker as eleven bells echo through the firehouse. Over the loud speaker, Captain Jack's voice bellows, "Roll call in the kitchen, rubbers."

"What am I gonna wear to roll call?"

"You really gotta loosen up."

"In a frozen shirt?"

At roll call in the firehouse kitchen, Captain Jack sips a cup of coffee, trying not to dunk his mustache.

Frank cleans shrimp.

I enter and Frank says, "Welcome to the kitchen, now pick up a knife and get to work." A couple of minutes later John enters wearing a wet, work duty shirt. I can't help but chuckle.

"Is it raining in here?" Frank asks.

"Let's get down to business," Captain Jack says.

13

"Your positions for the night-tour are: Frank – you're driving, John – Outside Vent, Billy – Roof. I'll be in my office, so don't go in there."

The captain heads to his office as John and I grab a pile of shrimp to clean.

I look curiously out the front, firehouse window. "Frank, when you drive the limo to work you take up two parking spots. I had to park a mile away."

"My car is in the shop. I had to take the limo."

"How's business?"

"It's a little slow this time of year but prom season is right around the corner."

Frank has another job driving a limousine to make ends meet. Actually, he owns the limo, and it's a business for him. Like many businesses, it's seasonal. May through October are his bests months because of proms and weddings.

"If you know any high school girls that need a date for the prom, let John know," I joke. "He hasn't had a date in months."

"Billy's still waiting for the photos on his locker to come to life," John says.

"I'm still waiting for you two knuckleheads to pick up a knife and get to work," Frank says.

"Madison Park is in town, and John's going to see a Jazz Penis."

"Pianist," John shoots back. After a moment of thought, John looks up from the shrimp, glares at me and asks, "Who's Madison Park?"

3

Fiery Fate

Now back to me, I wait impatiently backstage for the concert to begin when the huge concert hall goes dark and silent in anticipation. Then colored, laser lights, suddenly, flash wildly and a controlled explosion rocks the house. Thousands of teenagers challenge their lung capacity as Madison Park storms the stage. She sings her hit song that tells the passionate tale of a cheating, ex-boyfriend – as if she knows what real passion is. Maddy is an amazing dancer. Of course, she learned to dance before she learned to walk – which could explain why she's such a klutz. But the way she dances, you would never know it.

Angie and I watch every concert from start to finish just off the side of the stage. We have different reasons for it though. Angie narrates her daughter's performance as if she's feeding her the dance moves, but she's just a control freak. Me, I'm the biggest Madison Park fan in the world. Actually, that's not fair. Angie loves that girl more than anything in the world. She just gets caught up in the business side of things and forgets she needs to be a mom as much as she needs to be a manager.

If you could see me now you would see that I am flawlessly kickin' it hardcore right along with Maddy. Of course, I'm off stage but sometimes I close my eyes and imagine I'm out there rockin' it right beside her. I should be on "Dancing with the Stars" except I'm not a star – but I am. Okay, I admit, it's a little weird that I know every dance step and every word to every song but realize I spend a lot of time with this girl. I'm her life coach, remember.

As for Angie's psychosis; a cigarette dangles from her lip while she mouths her daughter's moves, "Step left and right and spin, arms raised and bow."

When the set ends, Madison storms off stage past Angie and me. She makes a b-line to her dressing room, to get ready for the next set. Her long strides enhance her perfectly sculpted legs as her wavy, blonde hair floats in the air behind her. Her hips are perfectly proportioned to her boobs, which are too big for her small frame but far from too big. She breezes by me like a sexy bullet.

"Slow down, Flo-Jo," I shout. "What's your rush? You sure as hell ain't picking out your outfit or puttin' on your own makeup." By the time I catch up to the girl, she's in her dressing room.

"You were amazing out there," I gush.

Angie enters lighting another cigarette and agrees, sort of, "You were terrific but what happened to that side step?"

Madison spins her head around with dramatic purpose, "What?"

"You missed a step. The side step coming off the front spin."

This is gonna get ugly.

"What did I say about smoking around me?" Madison says, shifting the focus to Angie's shortcomings. "Haven't you heard the reports about second hand smoke?"

"I'm always around you."

That's true, the poor girl hasn't had alone time since she was in the womb.

"Did you tape my show for me?" Madison asks.

She knows the answer is only going to disappoint her – but maybe that's what she wants.

"What show?" A clueless Angie replies.

Here comes the ugly.

Madison whips her head around again – which is unacceptable as I'm trying to work. So I stomp my foot theatrically and scold her, "Maddy, don't move so much or I'm gonna end up tying your hair in a knot."

"I asked you to record my show, 'A Wedding Story'," Madison fumes. "Did you?"

Angie isn't humble enough to admit she forgot, despite the fact that she's juggling concert bookings, media appearances and charity brunches. It's hard managing the career of the girl everyone wants.

"Goddammit!" Madison shrieks. "You can't even do the one thing I ask. It's a lousy Tivo machine. All you have to do is push a button."

Angie's only defense is a strong offense.

"Why are you so fascinated with ordinary people getting married? Your wedding is going to be a hundred times more grand than any wedding you see on that show."

"My wedding? Are we going to be able to squeeze it in between concerts and promotion appearances?"

"Madison Park!"

"Don't 'Madison Park' me. I'm not a child anymore. And don't talk to me about my wedding when I only see my boyfriend twice a year."

Angie is ready to bail out of the conversation with the understanding that she's just not going to win. Besides, she has bad news that just can't wait. And

Maddy can only argue so much because she has to be on stage in three minutes so this is the perfect time to break it to her.

"Madison, I added a show," she says.

"What? Why? I told you I wanted some time off to see the sights."

I must interject here, "Girl, the only sights you need to see are Sak's Fifth Avenue and Bloomingdale's."

"Jorden is coming to see me and I'm spending the weekend with him. Cancel the show."

"Jorden's not coming, honey. He called this morning."

It's obvious Madison is trying desperately not to show how crushed she is at this very moment. I feel so bad for her I want to collapse to the ground, curl up in a ball and make my eyes rain for her.

"Why didn't he call me?"

"He always calls me when he cancels on you, honey," Angie reminds her. "He hates to disappoint you."

"Then why does he do it so often?"

"This is a great opportunity," Angie says. "The album is going to drop in a few weeks and since we now have extra time in New York we should take advantage of it by adding a show."

19

"You should have asked me first."

Angie is a pro at these moments; she knows exactly what to do – feed Maddy's ego. She calmly says, "The show sold out in an hour."

"An hour?" Even Madison is surprised. "That's got to be a record."

"They love you in the Big Apple," I can't help but add.

"You have the rest of your life to sightsee," Angie says.

The business-minded Aries in Madison takes over and she changes her tune, "You're right, it's just a bunch of tall buildings."

A stagehand wearing a headset pops in and informs us, "One minute."

"Is my song list ready and programmed?" Madison asks, as she springs out of her chair.

"Done," Angie assures her.

"You are one sexy rock star," I say, admiring my own work.

"The sexiest girl that hasn't kissed a boy in six months," she says, as she looks herself over in the full-length mirror. I feel her pain like it's my own so I sigh melodramatically as she says, "Tighten me up."

Then she bolts from the dressing room. I try to

keep up and make the final adjustments on her outfit. I never knew anyone that can move so fast in heels. It helps that she's been in them since she was four years old. She could probably run the length of a soccer field and score a corner kick from fifty yards out in those things. Let's see David Beckham do that. David Beckham, now that's a sexy man. Where was I? What's going on? That's right. "Wait up!"

While I'm chasing "lightening girl," Angie sits back in the dressing room to enjoy the rest of her cigarette, now that nobody's there to complain about it. Suddenly, Angie sees Madison's headset microphone on the dressing room table. Madison forgot her mic and she's gonna make a fool out of herself when the music comes on. Nobody will hear her.

Without taking the time to crush it out, Angie carelessly tosses the lit cigarette in the trashcan. She grabs the headset and bolts from the dressing room toward the stage. Angie's an old pro at running in heels too — someone had to teach Madison. She catches up to her just as I tie the bottom string on Maddy's leather bustier, and hands her the mic. Madison puts the headset on and plugs it in the little box on her hip just as the curtain goes up.

The spotlight shines and the crowd roars! How

21

can I stop myself from dancing? The music infects my brain – I'm under a spell as I shout, "Kick it, Maddy."

Angie stands stoic, studying every step Madison takes and every note she belts out. Is she smiling enough? Is she animated enough? Is she good enough? While Angie psychotically ponders so many little, nonsensical things a light haze of smoke wafts through the air. I, of course, am way too into the show to notice it. Angie smells cigarettes twenty times a day so she's immune to light smoke.

***

Mealtime is a very important time at the firehouse. Much like at any home, the meals are a time to bond. We're still cleaning shrimp in preparation for supper.

"After cleaning fifty shrimp, the last thing I want to do is eat them," John says, annoyed by the chore. "I don't even like shrimp to begin with."

"Don't say that or you'll have shrimp for dinner every night-tour for the rest of your career," I remind him.

"I take that back; I love shrimp," John says, reversing his position on the tasty lil' critters.

"Like it or not, you need to know how to season it, bread it, bake it, fry it and broil it – depending on what I'm in the mood for," Frank says.

"John will never make anything as tasty as my meatloaf stuffed with mozzarella cheese," I boast.

"I remember that meatloaf," Frank adds with a

painful look on his face.

"I'll never forget it," John says. "After a year and half it's still in my stomach."

"There was a lot of love in that meatloaf," I say, defending my masterpiece.

"There was a lot of something in that meatloaf," John says.

***

Madison is a Goddess as the crowd sings along to her upbeat hit about a boy from the wrong side of the tracks pursued by a little, rich girl with curly hair.

Suddenly, that small waft of smoke turns to thick, black smoke as the fire gets going. From behind the stage, suffocating smoke engulfs the back-up dancers. The dancers instinctively run off stage nearly knocking me on my cute, little behind. One of them grabs me and pulls me through a long, smoke filled tunnel that only a few moments ago was a simple hallway. Now it's hell on earth as I try desperately to hold my breath until I reach fresh air.

Not far behind is our big bodyguard carrying Angie. She's coughing and fighting the whole way. We finally reach a side, exit door. Thank the Lord! I thought we were gonna meet our maker. Wait, the door is locked. A cruel God he is. This is no way to die. I want to die quick and painless. I can't handle this. This

23

kind of stress will kill me – oh wait, the smoke and fire will probably get to me first. I scream as loud as I can. "Help, somebody help us!" I can use Madison's lungs right now.

Then I realize, oh my God, Madison?

***

We finally finish plating the food.

John happily announces over the loudspeaker, "Chow's on."

We sit down to eat when the tone alarm blares throughout the firehouse – "Bee-doop." How's that for timing?

The dispatcher is heard over the loudspeaker, "Report of a fire at nine sixty-five, Seventh Avenue – first due truck, first due engine." That means that we are going to be the first fire companies on the scene.

We bolt from the kitchen, slide the poles and arrive at the garage area. We put on our firefighting gear – also known as "bunker gear." Frank starts up the truck and everyone gets on. The trucks pull out of the firehouse with the sirens blaring, lights flashing and the air horn blowing. Barreling down the city street, cars reluctantly move out of the fire lane, making room for the fire truck.

Inside the truck, Frank tells Captain Jack, "Nine sixty-five, Seventh Avenue – that's the concert hall."

"Yeah, this could be bad," Captain Jack says.

The dispatcher says over the truck's radio, "Manhattan to Ladder Thirty-nine."

Captain Jack picks up the radio receiver and responds, "Thirty-Nine truck; go dispatch."

The dispatcher informs him of a "second source." That means that two people reported the same fire. It usually means we got a job. And by job, I mean a working fire.

"Second source," Frank yells to us in the back of the truck.

The dispatcher comes over the air with more bad news, "Ladder Thirty-Nine; be advised we're receiving multiple calls of people trapped. You're going to work, Thirty-Nine."

"We got a job," Frank yells again to clue us in, craning his neck.

Captain Jack picks up the receiver and acknowledges the dispatcher, "Ten-four."

John and I buckle up our bunker coats, tuck our protective hoods under our helmets and put our arms through the shoulder straps of our air masks. I raise a fist and give John a good luck pound as the truck pulls up to the concert hall.

Thick, black smoke pours from the main entrance as hundreds of teenagers run for their lives. We jump off the truck and Captain Jack barks orders, "John, Billy, go around back and force your way in if you have to."

John and I diligently follow the orders of our commanding officer and make our way around the back with our tools. John grabs a power saw, just in case. En route I open my air cylinder. As the air reaches the face piece it vibrates for a second and beeps three times as a self-test. John opens his cylinder and the face piece vibrates momentarily and beeps three times, also passing the test. We reach the back door of the concert hall where we hear people trapped inside. They're coughing and banging on the door.

John grabs the remote microphone of his handie-talkie, "Cap, we have the fire in the rear with trapped occupants. Transmit the ten seventy-five."

If you haven't figured it out yet, although, I'm sure you have, "ten seventy-five" is the code for a structural fire.

I stick my halligan tool – a long metal crowbar – in between the doors and try to pry them open. John immediately starts up the power saw, pulling the cord, like you would start a lawnmower. The saw starts right up and cuts through the lock on the door. I continue to force the door open. The diamond tip blade slices through the metal like a warm knife through soft butter. Sparks fly everywhere as the door pops open.

***

Finally, I'm outside breathing fresh air. OMG, I almost died. The back-up dancers burst through the open doors behind me as smoke pours out from over our heads. The big bodyguard carries Angie out. She's no longer fighting him as she's just glad to be alive – until she gets her bearings, grabs him and shouts in his face, "Get back in there and get Madison. You get paid to protect her, not me!"

The bodyguard looks toward the open door where heavy, black smoke pushes out. He freezes.

"Get in there," Angie barks.

The big bodyguard ain't goin' in that building and that's final. He's alive and he's gonna stay that way. It's called self-preservation.

***

John and I wait for everyone to file out. After the last person runs out, a woman grabs John and yells in his face, "My daughter's in there! Save my daughter!"

John peers at me and I raise my eyebrows in a "Mam. I don't think your daughter's gonna make it kinda way." But I don't actually say that, of course.

John's a bit more optimistic when he carefully assures her, "We'll do what we can." But he doesn't want to make any promises we can't keep.

We mask up and crawl in.

John crawls along the left-hand wall with his left hand out as a guide.

I'm on the opposite wall using my right arm to guide me as I keep it glued to the right-hand wall. Eventually I come to a doorway where I'm blasted with superheated smoke and gases. "This must be it," I think to myself. Although it's ajar I can make out a star on the door. Staying on the right-hand wall I crawl into the room. The far corner of the room glows bright orange with fire.

27

After a brief search of the room on all fours I'm shoved back into the hallway by the scorching heat. I grab the remote mic of my handie-talkie, pull my face piece to the side and call my captain, "Cap, I got the main body of fire. It's in a dressing room back here."

Captain Jack has his hands full with escaping fans at the front of the building as he responds over the air, "I'll have the engine stretch a hose line. Do you have control of the door?"

I pull the door closed to keep the fire confined to the room and respond, "Ten-four."

Outside the entrance where John and I entered, the engine pulls up. The engine company firefighters stretch hose off the back and hook up to a fire hydrant. The engine firefighters enter with the hose line. Eventually, they reach me at the fire room door and wait for water.

Back outside, the engine company chauffer opens a valve on the fire engine and the water flows from the fire hydrant to the fire engine and into the hose. They watch as the water surges through the hose until it reaches the nozzle at the door to the dressing room that's on fire. They're ready to go in. It's just in time as the fire laps out of the dressing room over my head. It has burned right through the top of the door.

John stays along the left-hand wall, as he is well past the fire. He knows it's never good to have fire between him and the exit. It's zero visibility due to the smoke, so if he loses that wall he'll never find his way back. The air on his back only lasts so long.

John comes to the end of the hallway when, suddenly, his mask begins to vibrate. The vibra-alert indicates he's running out of air. He grabs the remote mic of his handie-talkie and calls the captain, "Cap, I'm in the rear of the building. A woman told me her daughter's in here but so far my search is negative and I'm running out of air."

"Don't overextend yourself, John," Captain Jack responds over the radio. "If you gotta get out, then get out."

John starts to back out when, suddenly, he hears screams in the distance. He instinctively crawls toward the sounds. Now he hears horrible coughing. He's getting close, but he's almost out of air. He continues to crawl around, sweeping his arms across the floor when the screaming and coughing stops. That's not a good sign.

Now he's off his wall and deep into the building compounding the already sticky situation. He doesn't know what to do next. He's going to run out of air and he doesn't know where the victim is. Even worse, he doesn't know where he is. He lost his wall – his guide. He stops for a moment to try to get his bearings and decide what he needs to do at this moment.

Suddenly, out of the thick, black smoke, a figure jumps at him, coughing wildly. She manages to get out a few very important words in between coughs, "I can't breathe!"

Once again, John's rescuer instinct kicks in, and he puts her well being above his own. He takes his face piece off and – despite being unable to see – manages to fasten it to the girl's face. At first she pulls back because the face piece is still vibrating since the air tank is low. But it only takes a second for her to realize she's getting good, clean air that may save her life.

As for John, he pulls his protective hood over his mouth and nose for scant, but better-than-nothing protection. He realizes time is of the essence. He grabs the girl forcefully, as this is not a time to be gentle; lives are at stake. He leads her toward – what he hopes – is the exit. He grabs the mic of his handie-talkie and calls me, "Billy, I need your help."

I'm still at the fire room door. But now I'm on the hose-line helping the other firefighters put out the stubborn blaze. "I kind of have my hands full," I tell him.

"I need you to turn on your pass alarm," John says, over the radio. "I have a victim and I got turned around. I'm hoping the alarm can guide me out of here."

I press a button on my air cylinder and a loud alarm blares along with red, flashing lights. As long as he's not too far inside the alarm will act as a beacon.

John concentrates so he can zero in on the alarm. It's faint but he can hear it. He is further away from the entrance than he thought, but he knows which way to go, and that's all that matters. He focuses intently and follows the sound of the alarm, guiding the girl. As he moves, the sound of the alarm gets louder. Eventually, he can see the red, flashing lights. He realizes he's definitely going the right way and he's almost out. Finally, he reaches the dressing room where the other firemen are fighting the fire.

"Do you need help with the victim?" I yell over the noise of the hose-line.

"I'm good," John says, as he guides the girl out. Then, suddenly, the cylinder runs out of air. Apparently, he spoke to soon. In a panic the girl rips the face piece off, flailing her arms. She nearly lands a "left hook" to John's jaw, but he ducks at the last second. Then she tries to stand; not a good idea considering the heat over their heads is a thousand degrees. John acts fast, taking his left arm and chopping at the back of her knees. She immediately falls backward where John catches her with his right arm. He "duck walks" so he can move quickly but still stay low to avoid the searing heat. He heads toward the exit.

***

Outside the exit, Angie and I are a mess. Her daughter, my best friend is still in there. I close my eyes and silently pray for Maddy. Angie paces back and forth and mumbles incoherently to herself. For the first time in a decade she's not concerned about the pop star but she's genuinely terrified she may never spend another moment with her daughter. As the reality of the situation sets in, a lone tear rolls down her cheek.

Just as Angie has given up all hope, suddenly, a firefighter emerges from the building through the

31

thick, black smoke with a coughing girl cradled in his arms. She rushes over to the person in the firefighter's arms, recognizes her daughter, sighs and says, "Thank God, you got her."

Madison instinctively looks toward her mother for comfort after her near death experience, but Angie has already slipped into manager mode. She turns her attention to the paparazzo photographer, relentlessly snapping away, "Who gave you permission to shoot my daughter?"

Undaunted the photog continues to shoot, so Angie turns to the bodyguard, "What the hell do I pay you for? You were the first person out of there, and now you're standing around with your thumb up your butt. Do something about that photographer."

"I may have been the first one out but I was carrying you at the time – or maybe you don't remember," the bodyguard snaps back. Then he turns to the photographer and loyally does his job.

Madison breathes deep as if tasting fresh air for the first time. It's not just clean air she's experiencing; it's a new life, and she has John to thank for it. As he cradles her in his arms she can't help but to think about the last time a strong man held her that tight. She was nine years old and it was her father.

With tears rolling down Madison's soot stained cheeks, she looks at the firefighter's blue eyes – made brighter by the black soot on his face. She wants so badly to lay a huge thank you kiss on his lips. Instead, she coughs in his face, and then quickly apologizes in a raspy voice, "Sorry."

"It's okay." The firefighter cracks a shy smile.

Still nestled in his arms, they go back to staring into each other's eyes for a moment, when Angie approaches and says, "You can put her down now."

"Oh yeah, right," he says.

Madison grips him tighter in defiance. She's happy right where she is.

He carefully places her onto the gurney, to be loaded onto the ambulance. Then he turns to go, but Madison locks her hand in his and says, "Wait, you can't just leave me."

Suddenly, the photographer escapes the grasp of the bodyguard and snaps a photo of the firefighter and Madison, as she grips his hand tight and gazes into his eyes.

"I have to get back to work," the fireman says, ignoring the photographer. "And you need to go to the hospital and get checked out."

"What's your name?"

"John."

"Thanks for saving my life, John."

"Sure," he says, as he peers down at the death grip she has on his hand.

"Will you come visit me in the hospital?"

"Sure," he says.

Madison reluctantly lets go of his hand. The paramedics take over and wheel her to the awaiting ambulance. They lift her up and load her on.

John looks back, locking eyes with her one more time before the rear ambulance doors close, cutting them off.

4

"Press"-ed Into Action

At the hospital the next day, the nurses are frustrated by the amount of flowers they have to navigate to get from one room to another. They're everywhere. They line the halls from one end of the floor to the other. The elevator doors open to a "Ding." A doctor exits and has to step over a giant, floral arrangement just to get out.

It's just ridiculous inside Madison's private room. It's like a botanical garden. Personally, I love flowers. I can't help myself from admiring the different aromas, as I finish making-up Maddy. Even on a hospital bed she insists on looking good. I respect that.

Angie focuses on the electronic pages of her Blackberry. Madison sits quietly, which seems to be a frequent occurrence these days. But she has a lot to think about – like almost dying in the arms of a gorgeous firefighter. That's the way I want to go.

I know her well enough to know that she doesn't dwell on petty stuff like "near death experiences." But the gorgeous firefighter part would keep any girl's imagination busy for awhile.

Angie's Blackberry rings and she answers it.

I offer Madison water because I know Angie won't think of it.

Maddy summons me with one finger to lean into her so she can avoid raising her painful, raspy voice and asks me for a triple bacon-cheeseburger. The way she eats, it's a miracle she doesn't weigh five hundred pounds.

Before I get a chance to order the burger, she asks, "Do you think he'll come visit me?"

Honestly, I don't know who she's talking about.

Angie assumes she's talking about her boyfriend and says, "He's on the phone right now, honey. He was just asking about you." Angie is inappropriately flirtatious with him when she says into the phone, "I miss you too, honey. Hold on, here she is." Angie hands Madison the phone with a warning, "Be nice to him."

Madison folds her arms and strains her voice so he can hear her, "Just tell him to get his butt to New York. I'm in the hospital!"

"Talk to him," Angie insists.

Expecting to be disappointed and playing up the raspyness in her voice, Madison puts the phone to the side of her face and listens for a moment. "Fine," she says.

That was quick. But she still has the phone.

"Yes, that's all I have to say."

Not that it's any of my business but I don't believe that for a second.

Still on the phone, Madison squawks, "First, my birthday and now this! How could you not visit your hospitalized girlfriend?"

Here we go.

"I know you're busy. We're all busy. But I almost died." Raising her damaged voice elicits a nasty cough. She holds the phone away and tries to deal with the pain in her throat. One cough leads to another when, eventually, she catches her breath, calms herself, puts the phone back to her mouth, and accepts defeat. "Forget it," she says.

She pushes a button silencing the phone. Pushing a button hard on a Blackberry just doesn't have the same effect as slamming the old-school receiver on the big, triangular, square box. But that's what she was going for.

Angie immediately goes into defense mode, "He's working very hard on his solo career. Things have been hard for him since the band broke up. It's nice of him to call and check up on you."

"I almost died!"

"Oh, don't be so dramatic; you're alive and you're fine. The doctor said you'll be released in the morning. Now we focus on damage control." Angie walks over to the window and peers out at the paparazzi. "What are we going to do about this fiasco? We have to put a good spin on it. The doctor said your voice should be back to normal in a couple of days, but to rest it for at least a week. I'll cancel the Buffalo and Syracuse dates, and we'll stay here in the city."

"Why do we have to stay in New York?" Madison asks. "Why can't we go home?"

"You have to stay in front of the cameras, honey. You can't afford to disappear two weeks before the album drops. You know that. Step number one: we need to do something about the fireman."

I couldn't help but peek into Maddy's sad little eyes at this moment to see how she reacted to the very mention of him. And if you didn't have my "super-see-right-through-her-defenses-power" you wouldn't have seen it – but I saw it. She lifted her chin with a little more zest than usual, and her eyes suddenly had life to them.

"What about the firefighter?" Madison asks, pretending not to care.

38

"I'll write him a check."

That's Angie's solution to everything.

"What? How much am I worth?"

"Would you stop, Maddy." Angie explains, "We can't go wrong with cash."

I have to interject here, "You can't give a rescuer a cash reward. It's insulting. He won't take it."

"It'll be a donation to a charity in their name. That's great press."

Once she has an idea in her head, she goes with it, and nobody's gonna stop her.

"This ain't my first rodeo," Angie adds. "We'll make an event out of it. That'll keep you in the headlines."

"Wonderful, another press conference," Madison says sarcastically, as she sighs dramatically.

***

Two days later, out in front of the firehouse, a circus convenes. Not the typical wild animal circus but there are plenty of clowns – reporters, I mean. All the guys of Ladder Thirty-Nine and Engine Seventeen, including myself, await the casually-late Madison Park. I'm excited because I have a plan and considering John is my best friend, I feel the need to run it by him before I put it into action.

I pull John aside and say, "I've been on the job five years and the best I have ever pulled out of a fire was an old, fat guy. Nearly gave me a hernia. I could actually smell his body odor over the smoke. You, on the other hand, grab Madison Park, and you don't even know who she is. There is no justice in the world."

"Where are you going with this?" John says, showing no patience for the conversation.

"I read somewhere that she loves roses – red, pink, white, whatever – as long as it's a rose."

"Billy, you have to stop reading 'Teen-Beat' Magazine."

I pull a single, red rose from behind my back and show him.

"Where's the other eleven?"

"You're so naïve," I explain. "It's not about the flowers. A single, red rose is a symbol that dates back to Ancient Greece. The single, red rose makes the statement, 'I want to be romantic with you'."

"Wouldn't a dozen roses make the statement, 'I want to be romantic with you twelve times'?"

"Do you have any idea how much a dozen roses cost?"

"Actually, I do."

"Do you mind if I give it to Madison?"

"Why would I mind? I can't wait for this charade to be over with. I have to take a leak." John heads to the bathroom.

"Thanks bro, I owe you one."

As John walks off and disappears into the men's room, a reporter, Cynthia Santana, approaches me. Cynthia has dark hair and dark eyes and she's all business. I've seen her on the local, news, cable network. She's even hotter in real life.

"I'm Cynthia Santana, with 'New York News.' What's your name?"

"Billy Sullivan," I say with a seductive grin.

"Were you at the fire?"

"As a matter of fact I was at the seat of the fire. I pulled the dressing room door closed and contained the 'red devil' in one room – keeping it from spreading, thus allowing John and Madison to get out alive."

"John? You mean John Kelly. What's he like? Does he have a girlfriend?"

"Who cares?" I say, slightly annoyed. "I'm single and if you happen to mention that during the press conference, I wouldn't mind – if you know what I mean."

Cynthia smiles a mischievous smile and says, "I'll see what I can do."

I am so in!

***

I'm in the limo doing some last minute touch ups on Maddy's makeup and hair. We've been in the car for twenty minutes and Angie and Maddy haven't spoken a word to each other. Moments like this are absolutely excruciating. The tension is so thick I can hardly breathe.

Madison finally breaks the silence, "Why do I have to be a prisoner of New York? We've been on the road for six months."

41

"I've already explained this." Angie is growing tired of the same argument. "You need to rest so we can make up the concert dates. Flying back and forth across the country is not resting."

"You have me booked for appearances all week." Madison's voice is obviously coming back as she barks, "You call that rest?"

"You have to keep your face out there," Angie replies.

"What if I go visit Jorden?"

"He has a full week of rehearsals and concerts. You'll only be in the way."

"Were you ever in Daddy's way?"

Angie is briefly stunned and Madison uses the moment to plead her case, "Why can't we go home to Oklahoma for the week?

"Great idea, while you're there you can marry the sheriff, live in a two bedroom ranch and raise chickens for the rest of your life."

"What's wrong with that?" Madison asks, knowing it will anger Angie.

***

We are still waiting anxiously for Madison to show up. Okay, I'm a bit more anxious than everyone else. Finally, the white, stretch limousine pulls up. John hurries back from the bathroom just as Madison's limo

42

parks alongside Frank's limo.

***

Thank God we're here. I have to get out of this car. I can't take it anymore. I leap out first, free from the claustrophobic grasp of the mounting tension. Angie climbs out behind me and is annoyed by the presence of the other limo – as if it somehow diminishes the spectacle of our grand arrival.

Madison steps out after Angie with a dozen, red roses in her hand. From the smile on her face you would never know how uncomfortable the ride over was. As soon as she looks up, she locks eyes with John, who suddenly realizes his fly is open. He reaches down to zip his fly as a photographer snaps a picture.

For a moment, it's as if the two are mentally transported back to that magical moment in time. Listen to me, I sound like a fairy tale. But this is no fairy tale; this is real life and what I see in their eyes is that they want to jump each other's bones right here, right now, in front of everybody. These two young, beautiful people want to press their perfectly sculpted bodies together until they're swimming in each other's sweat! At least that's what I'm getting from this quick glance.

On the flipside it could be more like Madison

is thinking that John should have zipped his fly before she arrived.

Madison hands John the flowers. Flash bulbs pop relentlessly.

"Roses, my favorite," John says sarcastically.

Madison smiles, not sure what to think of the comment. "Thank you for being strong and brave. You saved my life and for that you get a copy of my new CD," she says.

"That's not all, of course," Angie adds, jumping in.

The bodyguard hands Angie and Captain Jack a large check for them to hold up for the cameras.

Angie presents the check, "Madison Park Incorporated presents to the Ladder Company Thirty-Nine, Fallen Fire-fighter's Fund this check for fifty thousand dollars. Thank you for your bravery."

Once again the flash bulbs pop one after another in rapid-fire succession when Cynthia Santana shouts from the crowd of reporters, "What is Madison going to do for John?"

"This is more than generous," Captain Jack says.

"I'm not talking about money." Cynthia holds up a newspaper with a front page picture of John and Madison holding hands and gazing into each other's eyes as Madison was being led to the ambulance, "It looks to me like a connection was made between the two."

Angie stutters, "I don't think-."

"How about dinner with the firefighter?" Cynthia asks.

John looks at Madison, embarrassed.

The other reporters back Cynthia up. "Yeah, why not?" A reporter shouts.

"One date," yells another.

Soon they're all pushing the issue, and John doesn't seem like a guy that gets pushed into anything – even a date with a hot, rock star.

He steps forward to put a stop to it when Madison suddenly exclaims, "I'd love to! I'm free tomorrow night."

I don't think John expected that.

I certainly didn't.

He looks at her to see what she's up to, and she has this huge, gorgeous smile on her face like she's the happiest girl in the world.

"What do you say, John?" Cynthia asks.

Talk about being on the spot.

John, suddenly mesmerized by Madison's radiant smile shyly answers, "Sure."

Truth is, despite the nice moment she and John had together, Madison is less concerned with making a love connection and more determined to piss-off Angie. And it's working.

Angie is as angry as Angie can be as she gives Madison a look like, "What the hell are you doing?" But Angie knows to keep it to herself right now.

I can tell Madison is loving every tension-filled minute of it.

***

"This is a disappointing turn of events," I think to myself, as I toss my single flower in the trash can.

***

Back at the hotel, after another tense car ride, I sit quietly waiting for the volcano to erupt.

"What were you thinking?" Angie finally asks, venting.

"Don't blame this one on me," Madison shoots back. "You're supposed to approve all the questions beforehand."

"I wasn't the one that blurted out, 'I'm free tomorrow night'."

"What did you want me to do; reject the lonely firefighter that saved my life – in front of a hundred reporters?"

46

"Yes!" Angie shouts.

"That would be good for my career," Madison says, adding a little sarcasm to bring home her point. "Isn't that what it's all about? I don't see the problem, anyway. He seems like a nice guy and it's just for publicity. What are you afraid of?"

I know the answer to that question and it's two-fold. One: Angie's afraid she's losing control of Madison but she sure as sugarplums ain't gonna admit it. Two: She's terrified Madison will fall for the blue collar firefighter.

"Just so you know," Angie says. "I explained the ground rules to those vultures. They knew what they were and weren't allowed to ask. That woman set me up."

"Actually, she set me up," Madison says. "And I'm glad she did. I could use a night out on the town."

***

That night, back at the firehouse, Frank pours himself a cup of coffee as I wallow in envy.

John casually eats a bowl of cereal.

Despite my jealousy, I'm happy for John. "You have a date with the hottest chick alive," I say, feeling the need to remind him.

"You know as well as I do it's a publicity stunt, not a date," John says, killing my buzz. "There's no

47

romance involved here. Why kid myself? I just want to get it over with." John finishes his cereal and leaves.

I turn to Frank, "I'd say he's a 'glass is half empty' kind of guy. I'm supposed to be the negative one around here, not him. John is happy-go-lucky. Please, punch me in the arm for saying, 'happy-go-lucky'."

Frank makes a fist.

"I'm kidding." I stop him. "You'll break my Ulna. It's annoying seeing him like this."

"He's heartbroken," Frank says, in John's defense.

"That was half a year ago. He's gotta move on and what better way is there than to score with Madison Park?"

"You have a point. It's about time he got back on the horse. But I don't think this is the way to do it."

"What? Why not? She's hot!"

"You're not as stupid as you look. You know as well as he does the whole thing is a sham. You just can't get your mind out of her panties long enough to admit it. It's a publicity stunt. He's being used. How would you like being used?"

"Actually-," I say with a smile.

"Forget I asked." Frank refills his coffee mug.

I think for a moment and realize. "You and John are right. This whole thing is wrong – but I have an idea."

Frank's shoulders suddenly collapse as if he knows the diabolical plot I've just concocted in my brilliant mind is going to involve him. "Do you have a wedding or a prom tomorrow night?" I ask.

48

"No," Frank says.

"Are you thinking what I'm thinking?"

"If I'm ever thinking what you're thinking – shoot me."

"I need your help and you owe me a shift. Do me this favor – no, do John this favor – and we're even."

"What sick, twisted plot did you conjure up in that tiny, little brain of yours?"

I crack an evil smile.

5

And We Danced

The big night is upon us and John and Madison sit quietly in the back of the limousine as the big bodyguard drives. Quiet may be an understatement. It's like a quiet contest between the two, and they're both winning, except no one's winning. The uneasiness of the situation seems to force a small breath from John like a weak cough and Madison responds, "What?"

But John hadn't uttered an actual word. "I didn't say anything," he says.

"I thought I heard something."

"I didn't say anything. Maybe you said something."

"I asked you if you said something," Madison says.

"I mean before that," John explains.

"I didn't say anything. I thought you did."

"I didn't say a word." Now John's embarrassed and thinks he probably should have tried to make conversation.

"Okay," Madison says.

After another moment of awkward silence, John admits, "I might have coughed."

"That's probably what it was," Madison says. She suddenly realizes the situation is actually far more uncomfortable for John than it is for her. She feels she should warn him of the circus he's about to perform in. "There will be a lot of press at the restaurant. Pretend they're not even there. Just hold your head up, smile and walk right past them."

"I can do two out of three," John responds, with no intention of smiling.

"Just do as I do," Madison says confidently.

***

At the restaurant, a red carpet is rolled out and lined with reporters. Against Angie's best efforts, Cynthia Santana is one of them. She's with a man with a video camera on his shoulder.

The limousine finally pulls up to the restaurant. The bodyguard gets out, opens the limo door, and out steps John. He immediately turns to help Madison out of the limo. Madison is pleasantly surprised by John's manners, and she's taken out of the moment – just for a second.

Madison refocuses on the task at hand – smiling big. The spectacle rivals the Oscars as Madison steps onto the red carpet. John is visibly uncomfortable by the attention.

On the other hand, for Madison it's a typical night out. Angie patrols the perimeter of the carpet keeping the press at bay. Madison struts confidently down the velvet runway, when suddenly, a heel gets caught, and she trips and falls flat on her face.

John instinctively chuckles as he reaches to help her up. With his help, Madison gets to her feet.

"Are you alright?" John asks, trying to hide his smile.

"You think that's funny?" Madison angrily responds.

"A little," John says. "Do I have to do that?"

"No," she says, actually cracking a smile. "I'm such a dork."

Angie misses the whole thing, but Cynthia catches it and shouts, "Are you alright, Madison?" Before she can answer Cynthia shouts again, "How is the date going?"

"Very nicely," Madison says, playing the part. "My hero was a gentleman the entire ride over."

"What the hell does that mean?" John whispers, annoyed. "What were you expecting?"

"Let me handle this," Madison says.

The two continue down the red carpet and enter the restaurant.

The reporters are stopped at the front door.

Things are looking up for John. In fact, the restaurant has a full staff working, but the firefighter and the pop star are the only two eating.

Angie guides them to a table in the middle of the restaurant where the paparazzi outside won't be such a distraction. Before she goes over to the bar to pretend she's not looking over their shoulders, she says, "Enjoy dinner, it's on me. The limousine will pick you up right out front when you're ready to leave. It will take you to 'Posh'."

Another place where Angie can keep a close eye on them.

"Posh?" John says, scrunching his forehead.

"The dance club," Angie explains.

"I know what it is," John says. "Do I look like a dance club kind of guy?"

Angie couldn't care less what John likes or dislikes. "I'm sure you'll make the most of it. I'll leave you two alone."

"Somehow I doubt that," John says.

Madison smiles at John. She loves that he said that. She has yet to meet a man willing to stand up to

Angie.

Ignoring him, Angie walks over to the bar and pulls up a stool.

"So you don't like to dance?" Madison asks, initiating the conversation.

"I didn't say that. I said, 'I'm not a dance club guy.' But I can get funky with the best of them."

"Funky, huh? People don't use that word anymore."

"I do."

A much too serious waiter approaches with some form of food. "Please enjoy our succulent escargot," he says with a foreign accent.

"If it's free, it's for me," John says, excited to dig in. He takes a large forkful and shoves it in his mouth.

"Do you know what escargot is?" Madison can't wait to tell him.

"Do I want to know?" John asks with a mouthful.

"Snails," she says smiling.

John immediately drops his fork and downs a full glass of water. After they're washed down he says, "You had to tell me."

"Are you kidding? I couldn't wait but I wanted

to make sure you had a good mouthful when I did."

John smiles. He actually appreciates that. "I thought it smelled a little funky."

The waiter attempts to get their drink order, "Would you like to order something to drink? We have an extensive wine list."

"I'll have a Budweiser," John says smiling.

"Sorry, we don't serve Budweiser," the waiter says.

"No Bud? That's un-American."

"We have 'Maretti Red," the waiter says.

"Is it beer?" John asks.

"Yes, it's Italian."

"Italian beer? What the heck, I'll take one."

Madison watches the exchange but is more concerned about the power struggle she's having with Angie. She can't get over the fact that she had some time off and Angie would not let her see her boyfriend. Instead she's eating dinner with a stranger — although he's a cute stranger. And she's always happy to eat. But she's not gonna go down without a fight. She peers over John's shoulder at Angie at the bar when she gets an idea for revenge. Out of nowhere, Madison flirtatiously throws her hair back and laughs seductively, out loud.

"Did I say something funny?" John asks confused.

"Italian beer, that's so funny."

"Not really," John says.

Madison, again, laughs loudly and elicits the exact response she was looking for – Angie peers over at the table concerned Madison might be having too good a time.

"You're so funny," Madison exclaims.

"Whatever you say."

The waiter turns to Madison, "Would you like a glass of wine?"

"I think she's had too much already," John says.

"No thanks, just a Sprite."

John isn't finished ordering drinks, "Two shots of 'Soco'."

The waiter goes into his spiel, "As for the specials. . ."

John interrupts him, "Surf and Turf, medium on the steak, thank you."

"We have a fifteen ounce King Crab lobster and a twelve ounce filet mignon," the waiter says with a snooty attitude.

"Sounds like Surf and Turf to me." John smiles.

The waiter repeats the order, "The steak and

56

the lobster for the gentleman. And for the lady?"

"Let me guess," John says, "You'll just have a salad."

Madison is insulted. She feels the comment is an affront against all women. She says confidently, "Actually, I'll have what he's having."

The waiter repeats the order, "Surf and Turf for the lady." He leaves, and John takes the opportunity to get under Madison's skin, "You have to stop with that hero crap. It sounds stupid."

"What?"

"On the way in, you told the press, 'I was your hero'."

"You saved my life," Madison says.

"That's my job. And I have a name. I'm not a hero and I'm not 'the firefighter.' My name is John."

"Okay, John."

Not through being annoying, John lights up a cigarette. It's as if he's trying to sabotage the date. He has no idea how successful this maneuver will be.

Caught between trying to anger her mother and the powerful urge to yank the cigarette from John's mouth, Madison asks, "Do you ever get a girl to kiss you with cigarette breath?"

"Were you planning to kiss me?" John smiles,

knowing he's getting to her.

"You can't smoke in here. It's illegal."

John looks around the empty restaurant. "I don't think anyone is going to complain."

Madison gives up and flashes him a look of disappointment. Surprisingly, the look cuts right to the bone.

John feels like a jerk. He crushes out the cigarette and admits, "I don't even smoke."

"If you don't smoke, then why-?"

"Let's talk about you," John says, interrupting her. "I know this date is a sham. It's a publicity stunt for you, and it's free beer for me – free Italian beer – nevertheless, free beer. But you're playing this thing up a little much."

"What are you talking about?"

John mimics her as he whips his head back tossing his pretend, flowing locks and exaggerates a high-pitched giggle.

From the bar, Angie turns wishing she knew what the heck was going on.

"What's that all about?" John asks. "There are no cameras in here, are there?"

"No, there are no cameras," Madison says.

"Then who are you doing it for? I know it's not

me. What's your angle?"

Madison is busted but too stubborn to admit it, "I just want us to have a good time. Is that so hard to believe?"

John thinks to himself, "Yes, it is too hard to believe." But he wants to give her the benefit of the doubt. For an international super-star, she's pretty humble. In fact she seems like a pretty cool girl. Not to mention, she's ridiculously gorgeous. He'll never admit it, but he wants to believe that maybe she is doing all this for him.

The waiter returns with the drinks.

John raises a shot of 'SoCo' and says, "Do a shot with me."

"I don't think so."

"One shot – to a good time."

"Okay, one shot."

They both pound the shot.

Thirty minutes later, the table is littered with empty shot glasses as the food arrives. Their mouths water as the cranky waiter places the fancy plates on the table. Not one square inch of the table is bare.

"You're never going to eat all that," John says, eyeing Madison's food.

"Wanna bet?"

59

"Yeah, if you can't finish every last bit then we go where I want to go after dinner. And it's not going to be 'Posh'."

Madison agrees and reaches her pinky finger over the table.

John hesitates for a moment. "Not that I believe there's a snowball's chance in hell that you're going to eat everything – but, if you do?"

Madison smiles.

***

In a parking lot, a few blocks away, unbeknownst to anyone, a caper is being conducted. It's a symphony of romantic intrigue. The bodyguard sleeps soundly in the driver's seat of the limo, awaiting the call to pick up Madison and John. I peer into the window to confirm the man is in dreamland. Then I look around to make sure nobody is looking. I lie on the ground and slither under the limousine. While under the car, I pull a pair of wire cutters from my pocket and start snipping away at any wires I can find. I'm a firefighter not a mechanic so I don't really know which wire does what, but I know that if I cut enough of them, the car won't start.

***

Back at the restaurant, the front doors open, rousing the media. All of the reporters immediately leap to their feet and the flash bulbs pop. As they exit Madison looks beautiful as she smiles for the camera –

John is not so beautiful. He wears only his boxer shorts, socks and shoes as he waves a large, turkey leg for the camera.

Angie knows immediately Madison is behind this. She rushes up to them. "Where are his clothes?"

Madison looks over her shoulder toward the table as if to say, "Go fetch."

Angie runs inside the restaurant in a huff.

"I think they got enough pictures," John whispers to Madison.

"Not yet; take a bite," Madison whispers back.

John can't believe she's making him do this. But he made a bet and he lost, so he's gonna make good. He takes a bite of the turkey leg. In a strange way, he respects the heck out of her for this. As Madison and John approach the curb, the white limousine pulls up.

"Go ahead, take another bite," she says.

John doesn't like the request, but he's near the finish line so he tears into the drumstick with his teeth. Turkey skin dangles from his mouth as he furrows his brow like a caveman and raises the turkey leg high in the air. He acts as if he killed the bird himself. The flashbulbs pop.

Finally, John opens the door to the limousine and helps Madison climb in. Angie rushes over and hands John his clothing as he climbs in after Madison.

Inside the limo, Madison laughs hysterically and says, "I can't believe you actually did it. I guess you were still hungry."

"I should have put a little salt and pepper on it," John says, as he makes room inside the limo for Angie.

But Angie is stopped outside the limo by Cynthia, who shouts, "Are they still going to Posh?"

"They are going to Posh where they'll have a private ballroom and deejay all to themselves." As Angie is in mid-sentence, the limousine takes off, screeching into a u-turn at the intersection.

Inside the limo, Madison is tossed across the backseat and lands in John's lap – her face in his crotch. John's cotton boxers create a soft landing for her.

John smiles.

"Wipe that grin off your face," Madison says, looking up at him from between his legs. "This is a first date, pervert."

"I don't know what you're talking about," John says, laughing. He reluctantly helps Madison up and puts his pants on.

***

Angie stands in the street in front of the restaurant, stunned. The reporters are rather shocked as well. They're trying to figure out what's going on.

Angie immediately reaches for her Blackberry.

***

Oblivious to the current events, the bodyguard sleeps soundly when one of Madison's songs blares. It's the ring tone to his cell phone. Not the ring tone you would expect from such a big man. The bodyguard springs awake. He's still parked in the lot waiting for the call. He grabs his cell phone and answers. But before he can say a word Angie screams through the phone, "What the hell are you doing? Get back here!"

"I'm on my way," he says.

"You mean you're on your way back," Angie says, correcting him.

The bodyguard is confused by the comment but is focused on the task at hand – getting to the restaurant. He turns the key, already in the ignition. Nothing happens. He tries again – nothing. He realizes something is up.

"What the hell is going on?" Angie shouts, through the phone.

The bodyguard is too afraid to tell her.

63

Back in the other limousine, Madison realizes, "We left without Angie." She's suddenly nervous. It seems Madison doesn't realize how much she relies on Angie. She's like a crutch. Just then I lower the partition between the front seat and the back seat. From the front, I pop my head through as Frank drives.

"Hi guys," I say with a handsome smile – if I do say so myself.

"Billy, what are you doing?" John asks, as if it's not obvious.

"What's going on here?" Madison asks John.

"I don't know," John says.

"I'll tell you what's going on," I interject. "I'm salvaging your night. Consider me your guardian angel of good times."

"So you're kidnapping me," Madison says.

"Us," John reminds her.

"In a manner of speaking," I admit.

John orders me to stop the limo – as if I'm gonna listen.

I ignore him, so he goes over my head and tells Frank to pull over and he does.

Frank puts the car in park, looks over at me and says, "I told you it wouldn't work."

"I want out of this car," Madison demands.

"We'll take you back to the restaurant as long as you calm down," John says.

"Don't tell me to calm down, I'm being abducted."

64

"You're not being abducted," John says.

"What would you call it?"

John thinks about it for a minute and realizes, technically, she is being abducted.

"I'm doing this for your own good," I explain. "You two have the opportunity to have a great time, tonight. I can give that to you. I am the giver of great times. Just sit back and enjoy the ride."

"Take me back to the restaurant – now!"

"Why?" I shout back.

"Because this is crazy!" She says.

"You've never done anything crazy?" I ask.

Madison thinks about the question for a moment when John interjects, "Billy, take us back to the restaurant."

"Fine," I say in defeat. I'm not gonna waste anymore breath on them. I shouldn't have to convince them to have a good time.

The limousine retreats toward the restaurant when Madison's iPhone rings. It's obvious who's calling. Before she can answer it, John turns to her and says, "Maybe he has a point. I didn't want this date anymore than you did. I don't like being dragged around and put on display like I'm a small dog. I agreed to this to be polite."

"Nobody twisted your arm," she says. "I didn't know spending time with me was so horrible."

Her iPhone rings again as John opens up, "That's just the thing; it's not you. It's your mother, the photographers, reporters and fans. You're the only good part. You're confident, strong, pretty. You're not afraid to eat an entire cow in front of a guy you just met and you have a sick sense of humor. I love that. What do you say we take this ride and have a real date – just the two of us?"

The iPhone rings again.

Ignoring it, Madison asks him, "Why didn't you come visit me in the hospital?"

John is taken aback by the question. He forgot all about that. And he's surprised she remembered. He feels bad and doesn't know what to say.

"Well?" She presses.

"You were delirious. I didn't think you meant it." He opens up, "I knew who you were. Billy and I were talking about you earlier that day. You're a rock star; I didn't think you would want anything to do with me. Apparently I was right."

The phone continues to ring.

Madison is deeply impressed with John's vulnerability. But she wavers and says, "I can't date you, I hardly know you."

"This is how people get to know each other."

"It's not that easy for me. I can't just go out in public. I'd get swarmed by crazed fans."

At that very moment I lower the partition and reach my arm through. In my hand are a wig and big, dark sunglasses. Madison takes the wig, pauses and says, "I haven't been a brunette in a long time. But I'd rather have a bodyguard."

Her phone continues to echo throughout the

66

limo.

John looks at me, and I nod my head. The limousine stops abruptly and Frank gets out. The window goes down and all we can see is Frank's huge chest as he towers over the vehicle. Madison turns to John. "He'll do." She silences the ringing iPhone.

**

Back at the restaurant Angie is not sure whether to be furious at Madison or worried because she's not answering her phone. Just then the limo passes by and John and Madison wave as they pass.

Angie just stares, shocked by Madison's disobedience.

Cynthia turns to her cameraman and says, "We have to follow that limo."

**

As we speed past the restaurant Madison turns to John and asks, "Where are we going?"

John gives me a smirk and says to her, "I know just the place. It's quiet and low key."

**

The limousine pulls up to "Hogs and Heffers," a bar in the West Village of Manhattan. Music blares through the thin, front windows.

Madison sticks her head out of the limousine window and eyes the joint when a bra flies from the bar, whacks her in the face and hangs on her head.

"What kind of place is this?" She asks, removing

67

the bra from her head.

"It's not like that," John says. "You'll have a great time, I promise."

"I can't go in there – dressed like this," she says. She rips the gown at the knees making it an instant mini skirt. "Quentin is never going to forgive me for this."

***

At the front door, Madison stands behind John as if she can hide there all night. They greet the bouncer who gives me, John and Frank a pound. He's a firefighter, and works as a bouncer for extra money.

"What do you know; it's mister hero," the bouncer says to John.

"A hero's a sandwich," John replies.

"When's the big date?" The bouncer asks. But he doesn't give John time to answer. "You are so lucky, Madison Park is hot. You gotta hit that."

"Can we go inside?" John says stopping him abruptly.

"Sure," the bouncer says.

I can't help but chuckle at the faux pas.

As we enter, the bouncer peers at Madison as she strolls by him. You can picture smoke rising from his head as the wheels are not just turning, but grinding, to figure the situation out. Before his brain overheats, Madison pulls her sunglasses down slightly and gives him a playful wink.

"Sweet," the bouncer says.

John and Madison head to the bar. Frank and I head toward the other end of the joint in order to give the

68

couple their space.

The music is loud and upbeat. As they make their way to the bar I see Madison smile at John. He smiles back.

Hundreds of bras line the back of the bar as it's a tradition for girls to donate their undergarment at the end of the night. The bartender is a hot chick in jean shorts that couldn't possibly be cut shorter and a top that doesn't fit – yet fits perfectly. The bar is all about sexy and the bartenders represent that very well. She wears cowboy boots and a cowboy hat but the attitude is all New York as she asks, "What'll you have?"

"I'll have a Bud," John says

"Appletini for me," Madison says confidently, despite having no idea what it is.

The bartender stares at Madison for a moment, reaches into the refrigerator, pulls out two bottles and says, "Two buds it is."

John pays for the beers and hands one to Madison. She stares at the beer as if expecting it to magically change into an Appletini. When it doesn't she takes a big swig and says, "Not bad."

"King of beers," John says.

From across the bar I can't help but notice the "deer in headlights" look in Madison's eyes. It's as if she's been let out of a cage or released from prison and she just doesn't know what to do first. The sudden, unexpected sense of freedom seems to be overwhelming her as she soaks up the atmosphere of the rowdy bar.

"So tell me about yourself," John says, bringing her back.

Madison quickly goes into her autobiography and explains how she started doing local, beauty pageants when she was five. She was so successful, at age nine she and Angie traveled across the country to other competitions.

Eventually she focused on the singing and was picked for "Teen Team," a television program that aired on Saturday mornings. Most kids should be outside playing by eleven a.m. on a Saturday but those who weren't couldn't get enough of "Teen Team."

After five years, the show ended and she embarked on a solo career with Angie at the helm. The experience gained from Teen Team coupled with a natural star quality would prove enough to make her an icon. The rest is teen pop history.

I read a lot of "Teen Beat" magazine. That's our little secret, by the way.

"And here I am today," Madison says.

"That's a great story but I want to know about you not your career," John says, trying not to be rude.

But that's just the girl's problem – she is her career. I gather, she's trying to figure out how to be both Madison the woman and Madison the pop star, but it's a work in progress. And she isn't about to share it with John – yet.

"What do you want to know?" She asks.

John thinks it's obvious. But this is a very new situation for Madison and John sees it in her face. "I've met your mother but heard nothing about your dad. Do you have any siblings? Do you like chocolate? What's your favorite color?"

Madison fires off in succession, "The colors of autumn; chocolate is a gift from the Gods; no brothers or sisters which at one point caused a lot of stress between my parents, but that ended when my dad died. I was nine."

John can see the pain in her eyes at the mere mention of him, "I'm sorry, what was he like?"

"He was the most respected man in town. He was the sheriff but he also raised chickens. He loved his chickens. He hated beauty pageants but never missed one. He made sure I played at least one softball game for every beauty pageant I competed in. I hated softball but I did it for him. I would have done anything for him."

"How did he die?"

"I'd rather not talk about it."

"Of course, I'm sorry."

"You know Angie is my mother. How do you know that?"

"She was very upset at the fire; the kind of upset only a mother can get. You seem surprised."

She isn't. Despite the recent power struggle they're best friends. I was there too and I saw the look in her mother's eyes. She was terrified of losing her daughter.

"Is everyone having a good time?" An emcee shouts into a microphone, interrupting them.

"Yeah," the crowd shouts back.

71

"It's karaoke time, so get up here and sing."

John peers at Madison in an attempt to get her on stage.

"Don't even think about it," Madison says. She knows exactly what's going on in his head so she immediately shuts him down.

"Come on," John pleads.

"Do you even know any of my songs?"

"Honestly, no. But I figured you'll go up, not me. I've never seen Madison Park in concert."

"If I go up, you go up."

"Okay," John says, compromising. "I'll dance."

"What do you mean?"

"I'll be your back up dancer."

"Let me get this straight," she says. "I go up there and sing, and you're going to come up with me and dance?"

"I can do the 'Running Man' and the 'Cabbage Patch'."

"Really," Madison says. "I should be resting my voice but I have to see this."

They head up to the small stage area at the back of the bar. Madison turns to John and allows him to pick any song he wants. The song John picks is one Madison seems to be unfamiliar with, but being the professional she is, she picks it up right away. The song is "And We Danced" by the Hooters. It's an old, upbeat song from the eighties.

The old song finds new life with Madison singing it.

As the music plays Madison sings and John rocks back and forth as if warming up. Madison periodically looks back at him. Suddenly, John busts some crazy moves as Madison reaches the chorus, *"And we danced, like a wave on the ocean, romanced, we were liars in love and we danced, stepped away from the moment by chance – and we danced, we danced, we danced."*

The crowd is blown away by the performance. On one hand, Madison is amazing as she belts out the tune. On the other, John is hysterical, but surprisingly coordinated, as an over-the-top dancing firefighter. An instrumental solo in the song allows Madison to dance in sync with John. They bust out a crazy dance together. The crowd roars. I'm sure Madison is used to getting attention for her voice but by the huge smile on her face she's really soaking up the laughs.

Frank and I enjoy the show from the far end of the bar – that's when I notice the tattoo-covered, "rocker chick."

***

As the scene gets crazier inside, outside the bar is rather serene. It's a little later and there's no line anymore. Cynthia and her cameraman attempt to get in. The cameraman makes no attempt to hide the bulky camera on his shoulder. The bouncer immediately slips into brotherhood mode. He knows exactly what they're after, and he's not about to give it to them. With plenty of New York attitude, the bouncer asks them, "Are you kidding?"

73

"What?" Cynthia asks, playing dumb.

"That camera is not coming into this bar unless I smash it first."

"You can't threaten us," Cynthia says defensively.

"I didn't threaten you, I threatened the camera."

Cynthia realizes she's not going to win this battle. She retreats and huddles with the cameraman to devise a strategy. The cameraman tells her he has a very small, digital, video camera for times like this. It's a good camera and it's small enough to fit in a purse.

Cynthia is a pro and she knows how important it is to have pictures. Nowadays the media is ruled by video. These days it's not enough tell a story. You have to show it. She doesn't know exactly what's going on behind the doors to the bar but her instinct tells her it's the story of a lifetime.

After they put the large camera back in the van and grab the small one, they approach the bouncer again for another attempt to get in. The bouncer sees they got rid of the big camera but just isn't satisfied. It seems he's made a decision that they're not coming in – period. But Cynthia can be very convincing. She immediately falls back on her womanly wiles. The power she wields with her built-in, natural ability to seduce is downright magical. After a round of harmless flirtation, the bouncer bends.

"Okay, you can come in – but only you," he says to Cynthia. "The guy stays outside." Cynthia thinks for a moment. She couldn't care less if he goes in with her or

74

not. Her only concern is the small camera. He has it and she doesn't.

"Do you want your purse?" The cameraman says, to her surprise.

She doesn't have a purse, but the small camera bag can pass for one. The bouncer doesn't know the difference. It's a clutch move by the cameraman.

"I'll need money to buy a drink, right?" Cynthia says, taking the bag.

After the nice deed, the bouncer decides to make a move, "Maybe later we can grab a bite to eat at the diner."

"Maybe," she says with a seductive smile. She has no intention of meeting him later.

***

Cynthia enters the bar and is absolutely stunned by what she sees. Despite the disguise, she knows immediately that it's Madison on stage. Especially considering John is up there, dancing beside her. The two of them are putting on a great show and she's so excited she yanks the small camera from the bag, fumbling it to the floor.

She drops to her knees and fishes for it. Just as she reaches the thing it's kicked across the floor. Still on her knees, she scrambles for it when it's kicked again. As she gets close it's kicked a third time. Finally, she dives forward and falls on the camera desperately hoping it still works. It does. She pops up, reaches high and films.

A few feet away a scruffy, heavy-set guy is

75

enjoying the show, when he sees Cynthia next to him filming with the small camera. He recognizes her, "Aren't you Cynthia Santana?"

Cynthia denies it, but he knows better. He looks at her, then to the brunette with the powerful voice and big sunglasses performing on stage. The wheels are turning in the guy's head, as he moves closer to the stage to get a better look.

Madison and John come to the end of the song. The music stops and the crowd roars. Just as the applause dies down the guy recognizes the pop star, points at her and shouts, "That's Madison Park." The remark makes the crowd cheer even louder. In fact, they start to swarm the small stage.

Madison is terrified. She has no idea what to do.

Frank, at the bar, immediately tries to work his way toward the stage, but the crowd is too thick and out of control for him to get through.

John has to act fast. He looks for a back exit. He spots one behind the stage, grabs Madison, tosses her up onto his shoulder and heads toward the back door. They reach the door and exit the bar.

Out back, Madison is draped over John's shoulder. "You could be a little more romantic in lifting me up, you know," she complains. "Kevin Costner didn't heave Whitney Houston over his shoulder in 'The Bodyguard.' He cradled her in his arms."

"You're welcome," John says, as he gives her a playful spank on the butt.

"Whoa, first date remember!" Madison says.

Inside, Frank heads to the front door and helps the bouncer plug up the exit. Only problem is – Frank is the designated driver. He turns to the bouncer, "Can you handle this?"

"I got it," the bouncer says, as if this is a nightly occurrence.

Frank makes a mad dash to the limousine, parked right out front.

Madison and John round the corner to the front of the bar.

Frank jumps in the driver's seat. John opens the back door to the limousine for Madison, and she gets in.

Tho bounoor holdc off tho crowd and John waves to him to thank him. The bouncer gives him a thumbs up. By moving his arm off the doorframe for that split second the same rude guy that shouted Madison's name in the bar squeezes through and pops outside.

The guy who recognized Madison is face to face with John, who stands next to the limousine. Madison pokes her head out of the car door. The guy turns around, pulls his pants down, exposing his behind and shouts, "Madison, can you sign my butt?"

The rage make's John's eyes turn from crystal blue to fire engine red in an instant. He approaches the man who is currently in the process of zipping his pants, curls his fingers into a tight fist, pulls his arm back and belts him in the jaw. The guy falls hard on his back. Madison is stunned as the guy lies on the ground holding his nose.

John stands over him for a moment as if to say,

77

"Don't move."

When it's clear the guy has chosen to stay down rather than put up a fight, John turns, jumps in the limousine and shouts, "Take off."

Back inside the bar, everyone is jammed at the front door, trying to get a look at the pop star – everyone except me. I can see just fine through the front window. I don't expect I'll be able to get through the crowd and out the door so I go back to making-out with the "rocker-chick."

***

In the limo, it's silent for the moment. John reaches in the refrigerator and grabs a beer. The rude guy may have deserved it, but John still feels he should apologize to Madison, "I'm sorry you had to witness that," he says.

"I've never seen anything like that before," Madison says, a little shaken.

"You never saw a guy get punched in the nose?"

"Not in real life," she says. "Only in the movies."

"He deserved it. By saying what he said to you, he ran the risk of being punched in the nose. Nobody is going to speak to you like that when you're with me."

Madison is slightly shaken by the violence but she's impressed by the display of barbaric chivalry. She hasn't had someone stand up for her like that – who wasn't getting paid for it – since her dad died. Caught up in the moment, she leans in toward John who is somewhat surprised but more than ready for her. He closes his eyes wishing he had made the first move, but

78

he's certainly not gonna stop her.

She leans in close, when the limo comes to a sudden stop and Madison is thrown forward.

John opens his eyes to find Madison on her back on the floor. Her legs are up in the air and her self-created, mini skirt has ridden up her thighs exposing her panties.

"We really should start with a kiss," John says with a big smile. "Like you said, 'It's only our first date'."

"You're a real comedian," Madison says.

"Sorry about that," Frank says over the intercom.

"Where to now?" Madison asks.

John helps her up as she fixes her skirt. John is happy that she's noticeably more comfortable with him than she was before. But he's still a little surprised by the question, considering the way things ended at the bar. "You don't want to go back to the hotel?" He asks.

"Are you kidding me? This is the most fun I've had in years." She reaches in the refrigerator, grabs a beer, twists off the top and takes a big swig.

***

The limousine pulls up to a huge office building in downtown Manhattan. John wants some alone time with Madison. I don't think he expected the date to go so well. She made a strong impression on him so he naturally wants to return the favor by impressing her.

They get out of the limousine.

John explains to her how they get false alarms in this particular building all the time. These large buildings have automatic, smoke detecting systems that

79

sometimes work a little too well. They can detect a receptionist sneaking a cigarette in the stairwell.

In this building, the top floor is being renovated and the worker's tools create light smoke and dust that often set the system off. So we're there a lot. They enter the building, sneak past the security guard and duck into an elevator. John pushes the button for the elevator.

"Where are we going?" Madison asks.

"I want to show you something."

Inside the elevator, John uses his emergency, elevator key to override the elevator so it will bring them to the top floor that's being renovated. People get stuck in elevator cars every day in New York City. The key is used to take control of adjoining elevator cars, to get the people out of the stuck ones.

Madison thinks it's pretty cool that John wields power like that, although she has no idea what he's up to. The tension in the small space compels John to make a move. But he's too busy strategizing in his head about how to do it, and time is running out.

It's a long, quiet elevator ride as Madison thinks, "He's definitely gonna make a move."

John, on the other hand, is in these buildings and these elevators everyday and doesn't remember the ride being this long. He realizes he had plenty of time to make a move but, surely, it's too late now. With every passing second it gets more awkward until Madison – ever so slightly – leans in to John, resting her head on his shoulder and carefully placing her right arm around his waist.

John reciprocates by putting his left arm over her shoulder. She snuggles up to him, and John thinks to himself, "What a perfect time for the elevator to get stuck." Instead the elevator doors open. Of course!

They reluctantly get off. John holds Madison's hand and leads her to the window. Actually, the entire shell of the building is a window. They stand on a radiator that runs the length of the wall and lean into the glass.

"Don't worry, it's not regular glass. It's actually reinforced with alloy," John assures her.

Madison trusts him as she leans into the window. The view of the city is absolutely spectacular It gives the feeling like their hanging over the city.

John points out the different buildings and landmarks in the city. He can't help but notice Ground Zero so he points it out as well, without elaborating. It was a painful time for all New Yorkers, not just firefighters. All New Yorkers lost a piece of their heart that day. In fact, every American was deeply affected by that day.

I'm sure Madison understands why he doesn't say more, and she's certainly not about to press him. She just enjoys the wonderful freedom she feels at that moment.

After what seems like an endless amount of time soaking up the beauty of the New York City night-lights, John decides it's time to focus on Madison. He steps off of the radiator and away from the window. He takes her hand and helps her down. He looks her in the eyes,

takes the wig off her head and says, "You can lose this."
He tosses it aside and scans the floor. "Let's take a look
around," he says.

They wander the huge floor until they come
across a lone piece of furniture – a small piano.
Madison's eyes light up, "Look," she says. She grabs
John's hand and pulls him toward it.

They sit close on the piano bench.

John waits for Madison to play. She excitedly
pounds the keys, eliciting a terrible sound.

"What are you doing?" John asks.

"I don't play," she admits.

"Then stop – please. I'll show you how it's done."
John takes his two pointer fingers and plays Chopsticks.

"Even I can play Chopsticks," Madison says.

Just then, John transitions into an elegant
melody. The music is unfamiliar but echoes wonderfully
throughout the vacant floor. When John finishes
Madison looks at him in awe and says, "John Kelly, you
are full of surprises. That's a beautiful song, but I don't
recognize it."

"That's because you never heard it before. I
wrote it."

"Are there words?"

"I never wrote any. Honestly, I can't find words
good enough to match the melody."

As a musician herself, Madison understands.
"Besides, you don't sing," she jokes.

John smiles.

She smiles back, all the while thinking, "When is

this guy gonna kiss me?"

They gaze into each other's eyes again, setting up the moment that by now they are more than ready for.

Suddenly, the elevator "boops." The sound echoes throughout the floor.

A security guard with a flashlight gets out and looks around.

They duck beneath the piano as the beam from the flashlight passes over their heads a few times. As the guard searches, John leans into Madison, determined to get a taste of her lips. He goes for her bottom lip, which is the perfect size to sandwich between his. It's not big, but it's full. He loves a full bottom lip. Despite the footsteps getting closer and the flashlight getting brighter, the kiss is soft and slow. John runs his right hand through her hair. He gently cups the back of her head, while carefully but passionately pulling her into him, pressing his lips against hers.

Suddenly they feel a light on their faces. They reluctantly pull their lips apart and look up at the security guard.

"Can we have a few more minutes?" Madison asks.

***

John and Madison stand on the South Street Seaport and watch the sun come up over the three East River bridges: The Brooklyn Bridge, Manhattan Bridge and Williamsburg Bridge. It's an awesome sight. It makes Madison feel downright foolish for ignoring the beauty of New York for so long. She wonders what she missed in all the other cities she has so blindly passed through.

She thinks, "What a wonderful gift it is when a boy can show you such beauty." She looks at John and suddenly feels grateful that she didn't pass this by. John looks into her eyes for a moment wondering what's going through her head. He wants to ask but it's just not a thing guys do.

Just then, Madison asks, "What are you thinking?"

John chuckles at the irony of the fact that he was thinking about asking her what she was thinking but he doesn't tell her that. He says what every guy says, "Nothing."

But she knows it's something. She can feel it too. They go back to gazing at the rising sun.

***

It's morning and the limousine pulls up to the hotel as thousands of New Yorker's fill the streets, scurrying to work. John gets out, offers Madison a hand and walks her to the front door. She thanks him for a wonderful time.

John suddenly remembers something. Slightly embarrassed, he asks Madison, "Can I have an autographed picture for my little sister?"

"Your little sister, hah?" Madison says, as if she doesn't believe him.

"Apparently, she's a big fan of yours. She texted me tonight and asked if I could get her one."

"Of course, I'll have it delivered to the firehouse."

"I'd love to show you more of the city if you'd like. I'm off the next couple of days," John says.

"I have appearances; like promotion stuff," Madison says, genuinely disappointed.

"Of course you do," John says.

One part of Madison wants nothing more than to spend every waking moment with him; the other part of her is an international pop star.

Suddenly, Angie storms out of the hotel, points at Madison and says, "You, upstairs."

Madison turns and shoots Angie a look that would kill an average person. But Angie is not your average person, although she is about to find out that the apple doesn't fall far from the tree.

"I'll be up when I'm ready," a mortified Madison responds.

Angie is stunned by her daughter's petulance.

At that moment a car screeches to a halt right in front of the hotel. Four Paparazzi jump from the car and flash bulbs pop. It doesn't take long before the annoying "stalkers with cameras" start appearing from all directions. It's like they're falling from the sky.

The perpetual flashing blinds John.

Madison realizes she's running out of time before they're swarmed and John freaks out. "Maybe I can cancel something," she says.

"Maybe?" John responds.

"Absolutely not," Angie barks. "You have to get inside." She tries to get between Madison and the cameras.

John realizes that Angie, suddenly, thinks it's bad for Madison to be seen with him. "Forget it." He's had enough. "I don't know what I was thinking."

Madison struggles to choose between John, Angie and posing for the cameras. She backtracks, "I'll clear my schedule. It won't be a problem."

"Oh, yes it will!" Angie says, waving her long, bony, index finger.

"Shut up and leave us alone!" Madison shouts.

Suddenly the flashbulbs stop. Madison peers at all the frozen paparazzi and thinks exactly what they're thinking – they just snapped a front-page picture of Madison Park totally losing it.

"Just forget it, I have to go." John turns to walk away.

"Wait." Madison shouts.

John turns so that they're face to face and tells her, "Madison, you're one beautiful clown but I don't want to be a part of the circus."

John walks away.

The hurricane of emotions that flood Madison are about to be unleashed on one difficult person. You guessed it: Angie!

***

A door slams and I jump out of bed. I immediately think, "Drama!" Despite the fact that I insist on ten hours of sleep a night, I must find out what's going on. I'm in the room across the hall from

86

Madison. It's imperative that I be that close. If there is ever a makeup or wardrobe malfunction I can't be too far away. I peek out of my room door and see Angie and Madison enter Madison's room. I immediately go into the hallway with a glass, put it to the wall and listen. And yes that works – trust me, I know.

The moment they enter the hotel room, it's Angie who gets in the first word, "What the hell was that all about? I've been up all night worried sick."

"I called you three times from my iPhone," Madison says, restraining herself – for now.

"That doesn't make it any *less* dangerous for a girl like you."

"A woman like me," Madison corrects her. "And since when did you decide to be my mother again?"

Angie doesn't respond, as she absorbs the hurtful comment.

I cringe.

Madison suddenly decides Angie's not worth the energy of the argument and calmly says, "From now on, I'll make my own decisions regarding my life."

"Oh really," Angie scoffs.

"Really," Madison says confidently. "Cancel my appearances. I'm sleeping in."

"You can't do that. We have Z-100 radio station in one hour."

"Not anymore." Madison heads into the bedroom, closing the door behind her.

I think to myself, "What is going on?" I head back inside my room just in time because at that moment Angie storms out of Madison's room.

I feel the need to console Madison so I go across the hall. I notice her bedroom door open just a crack so I peek in. I see her sitting on the bed with a photo of her and her dad in her hand. In the photo, he has his sheriff uniform on as he holds Madison tight against him. They both smile for the camera. She stares at the photo and says, "I'd give it all up for one more hug." I feel it's best to leave her alone so I retreat to my room.

6

Jorden Who?

Across the country, on a beautiful California day, Jorden Vanderpool wears a geographically inappropriate, turtleneck sweater with sleeves that are too long for his arms. He has a trendy, blonde haircut and wears stylish glasses despite having perfect eyesight. He rehearses for his next performance as he sings and dances. To give you a glimpse into Jorden's persona, I'm initially inclined to call him a boy band alumnus but the truth is he never really graduated. The boy band was the pinnacle for him. It's like he's the most popular kid in high school except everyone, but him, moved on to college.

Of course he never went to high school; he was too busy being in the most popular boy band in the world. By the age of seventeen, he achieved more success than most will in their life but being washed up at twenty-one is devastating for a guy like him, and it's just not something he's willing to accept.

From the side of the stage, Jorden's agent, Steven Stanton watches carefully. Steven is a chubby, balding, wormlike creature that cares only about money – his money. It's apparent Steven is preoccupied with something. He's even more fidgety than normal.

Jorden nails the closing dance step when the song ends. Steven calls him over so he can have a word alone with him. Steven paces back and forth, visibly distressed. "Look at this," Steven says, as he flicks on the television.

In slow motion, a smiling woman splashes warm water on her face. It's a commercial for facial cream.

"I moisturize everyday with 'Lilly's Lovely Lavender Lotion'," Jorden says. "I'm not getting lines am I?" Jorden looks for a mirror.

"Not that; keep watching."

The commercial ends and Jorden stares when Cynthia Santana comes on, "We're back and just like we promised we have steamy footage of Madison Park and New York, firefighter John Kelly getting down and dirty at the famed Manhattan dive, 'Hogs and Heffers'."

The footage from the small, digital, video camera plays surprisingly clear on the television as Jorden watches John and Madison have the time of their lives on the small screen. Cynthia caps the story with, "Singing, dancing, flirting, oh my. What would Jorden Vanderpool say?"

"What would Jorden Vanderpool say?" Steven asks with an attitude.

"Jorden Vanderpool would say, 'so what,'" Jorden says in the third person with just as much attitude.

"That's supposed to be your girlfriend."

"Relax; Angie said it was a publicity stunt."

"Does that look like a publicity stunt to you? Did you see the smile on her face? I've got news for you, Jorden; she never smiles like that when she's with you. That's no stunt. That's on every celebrity, news show: TMZ, Entertainment Tonight, Inside Edition, Access Hollywood. It's making you look like a fool. Can't you see that?"

"What do you want me to do?" Jorden is starting to get annoyed.

"Go to New York."

"That's impossible," Jorden scoffs. "We have a tour to finish."

"It's not your tour. You're one of several opening acts. You're not the main event anymore – at least not here. But in New York, you will be."

"I don't need her," Jorden insists. "I can do this myself. I'm working my way back."

"Madison's last album went platinum," Steven says. "The new one is expected to go double platinum; you have to be a part of that album. I wrote a song with a musician friend of mine; it's a duet. You can sing it with Madison."

"I can sing it alone! Why does it have to be a duet?"

Steven tries another route, "How about a reunion tour?"

"Absolutely not. I'm a man and you can't make a boy band with grown men."

From nowhere, Steven drops a bombshell. "You've been dropped from the tour."

"What? That's impossible." Jorden is stunned. "They can't do that."

"They can and they did. I had to fight tooth and nail just to get you on it. If I could stand the sight of children, I would have to sell my first born to keep you on it." Then Steven ponders, "Come to think of it, there might be money in that."

"This is wrong," Jorden says, dejected.

"Right or wrong, it's reality. You're off the tour. The comeback is over. The solo artist is dead before he can live. It's better this way. We're losing money every day. You're not even getting paid enough for daily expenses. Forget about paying three mortgages and four car payments. If you want to have any future in this business you'll get on a plane to New York, win Madison back and maybe I can work something out with Angie about getting the duet on Madison's new album."

Devastated by the news, Jorden sits.

"If you want to keep the summer house, the ski lodge, the ranch, the Porsche and the three Humvees, you'll get on a flight to New York tonight. Otherwise it's back to the trailer park for you."

"I already lost the summer house."

***

The fire truck cruises down Fifth Avenue as John and I soak up the perfection that is the holiday season in New York. It's hard to explain the feeling and the best word is overused but appropriate – electricity. And, in fact, it starts with autumn. Fall brings that excitement that carries through the holiday season. Even two tough guys like us can sit across from each other in silence and just appreciate it.

***

Inside her hotel room Madison sits quietly as I work with her hair and let me tell you this is going to be hard. The hair is where I start and if she's not talking then this morning is going to drag. I need to talk. I had a Grande Mocha with an extra shot of espresso, and I'm gonna start speaking in tongues like a horror movie if she doesn't start first. The problem is, I have nothing to talk about. Okay, that's never stopped me before, but she has some juice and I'm thirsty.

Just then, from outside, a siren blares accompanied by a loud, air horn. Madison jumps up, rushes to the window and watches the fire truck go by. So that's what it is. I can't believe I didn't pick up on this. I must be losing it. By "it," I mean my super, special, intuitive powers of knowing exactly what's going on in her mind at every waking moment. She's smitten and I can't believe I just used that word. I knew it was good but not this good.

As Madison stares out the window, I use my best inquisitive tone and ask, "Is that Ladder Thirty-Nine?"

She drags her cute butt back to the chair and says, "No, I couldn't see the number, but it was an engine – not a ladder truck."

"And what's the difference?"

"Engines have the hose and ladders have the big ladder on it."

That makes sense, I guess. But I'm not interested in firefighting procedures.

Madison, again, stares quietly into the mirror.

"Maddy, I can't take this anymore; you have to talk to me. I'm starting to get worried. If you don't start talking I'm gonna call nine-one-one."

She peers at me through the mirror with a seductive smile, "You promise."

It's all crystal clear now.

"This boy had some effect on you."

"We snuck away," she finally admits.

"You what!?"

"Don't you watch T.V?" She says, scrunching her left cheek.

I look at the television, dying to put it on. But then it dawns me, I have the horse right here so she better open her mouth and spill it. "I thought Angie had this whole thing controlled. She's slipping."

She finally confides in me, "Last night I had a real date with a cool guy – like any normal girl."

"In a chauffeured limousine and a five thousand dollar, Vera Wang gown."

"About the gown," she says sheepishly.

"Tell me you did not desecrate Vera."

"Consider it a mini-gown now."

95

I inhale deep to stave off the shock and horror and keep from passing out.

"I looked good," Madison boasts. "He couldn't stop staring at my legs."

"You slut." Someone has to defend Vera.

"We talked and talked and talked some more. And not about record sales or concert dates but about food and hobbies and family. We played the piano and danced and drank beer and got in a fight."

"Time out, I can't believe such craziness, stop right there." I wave my hand wildly in the air to bring the conversation to a halt and ask, shocked, "You drank beer?"

"Budweiser. It's the King of Beers."

"But you don't play the piano."

"He does," she says. "We ended the date watching the sun come up at the seaport. I haven't had that much fun since. . ."

She actually can't remember a time when she felt as alive as she did last night. I know what you're thinking, she performs in front of fifty thousand people night after night and that sounds pretty exciting but the truth is, like everything else – it gets old. Most beautiful twenty-one year olds don't cry themselves to sleep at night because the loneliness consumes them.

"When do you see him again?"

"We didn't set anything up."

I shake my head violently but rhythmically from left to right to left and ask, "Why not?"

"We're from different worlds," she explains meekly.

You should see the face I'm making right now. "What does that mean? Is he a space alien or something?"

"No," she says, actually answering the question.

Suddenly, I see the upside "That's too bad; if he were a Martian he might have a really long tongue."

"Quentin!"

"I don't see what the problem is."

"It's not what, it's who?" She finally admits.

"So you're not going to pursue the firefighter because of an imaginary boyfriend?" Okay, technically, he's real, but he's never around and he's never treated her right. Quite frankly, he doesn't deserve her.

"I can't pretend he doesn't exist."

"Look around you. Do you see a boyfriend? No. Then he doesn't exist."

"That's not nice."

I think for a moment, considering whether it's

better not to interject my thoughts. After all she should live her life. Naaa! "The singing sap doesn't rock your world. He never has. When was the last time Jorden looked at your leg like it was a lollipop?"

Maddy actually likes the analogy and smiles for a moment as she thinks about the firefighter using her leg as an afternoon snack. She shakes her head and says, "I'm not sure he ever has."

"He's a comfortable old shoe. Eventually comfortable old shoes have to be donated to make room for the new Steve Madden's."

"You want me to donate my boyfriend?"

Actually, I was thinking he should be tossed out with the trash but there are lines even I won't cross. Madison tries to defend him but a woman as smart and sexy as Madison Park deserves better. Hell, she should have a man on a leash (one that doesn't poop on the sidewalk, of course). "I have one question for you." I pause for dramatic purposes then I simply ask, "Do you want to see him again?"

Madison hesitates because we all know the answer but she's afraid to give it so I have to pry it from her, which I am perfectly capable of doing. I spin her around so there's no mirror between us, kneel down and share with her something my grandmother

98

used to say, "If you're living in fear, you're not really living."

***

Frank backs the fire truck "into quarters," as the firehouse is called, while John and I hold up traffic.

I can't keep mute any longer; "I gave her to you on a silver platter. I can't believe you didn't close the deal."

"Is that what it was all about?" John asks. "Getting laid?"

I give him a look like he just asked me the dumbest question in the world, then I state the obvious, "Yeah!"

"Why do you care so much?"

"Because I'm jealous," I painfully admit. "Or at least I was jealous until you proved I had nothing to be jealous about."

"You did pretty good last night," John reminds me.

"I did?"

"You don't remember?"

"Was she hot?"

"Who said it was a she?"

"Oh my God, not again!"

"Billy, I was joking. What do mean, 'Not again'?"

I have to change the subject quick. "We're talking about you, here. You had a golden opportunity."

"It wouldn't have gone anywhere."

"Where did you want it to go? Don't you

99

understand, this was your one shot and you blew it. Why couldn't you just seize the moment – 'Carpe diem'."

"That means, 'Seize the *day*.'"

"You had Madison Park alone in the back of a limousine and you didn't have pants on. How do you screw that up? You'll never have another shot at her again."

At that very moment a white, stretch limousine pulls up and double-parks right alongside Frank's limo. I watch stunned as Madison gets out and approaches us. She greets me first, "Hi Bobby."

"Billy," I say, correcting her.

She turns to John, "Hi."

"You can stop staring and go inside now," John says to me.

I am frozen by her hotness but I snap out of it and head into the firehouse.

Madison hands John a large, yellow envelop, "I brought the picture for your sister. And there's one in there for Billy too."

John thanks her and expresses how thrilled his little sister will be. They stand on the sidewalk in front of the firehouse for a few moments chatting about nothing. The truth is, neither of them want to make the first move. And as Madison turns to go, it becomes apparent that she's going to chicken out.

But then she's suddenly filled with bravado, and turns back to John and says, "Just so you know, I cleared my schedule for the week. You can take that anyway you want. I guess, what I'm saying is; I've been

100

to New York fifty times and I've never seen the Empire State Building."

John hesitates. He doesn't like the attention Madison brings along with her. He's a simple, private guy and he wants to stay that way.

The bravado is wearing off as John stalls. Madison's like a rock on the outside, while inside she's a mess. But now that she's put it out there she's gonna go all the way. "I'm not taking no for an answer," she says.

"Oh, really," John says smiling.

Madison nods, remaining firm.

"I guess it's settled then," John says, finding her stubbornness adorable. "I'll pick you up tomorrow at noon."

"Perfect." Madison smiles in relief.

"Dress comfortably," John adds.

Madison smiles at him, not really sure what he means. Women don't consider comfort when they dress. He has a lot to learn. Madison heads back to the limousine, focusing all her energy on not tripping.

John waits for her to get into the limo. He's not a cocky guy but he can't help but think, "Who's better than me?" He's just had one of the hottest chicks in the world ask him out. Millions of guys would kill to have a date with Madison Park, and he's going on date number two. He can't help but come to the obvious realization that he's a stud.

Madison has one gorgeous leg in the limo, and John intently gazes at the other when she turns to flash him a smile and wave goodbye.

John, the stud that he is, smiles back, as a wave of water falls from the roof and crashes down on his head soaking him from top to bottom.

John shakes like a dog and removes the hair from his face just in time to see Madison laugh. She gets in the limo.

John is a little more humble now, quietly saying to himself, "Yeah, I'm cool."

On the roof of the firehouse, I hold an empty bucket with one hand and hi-five Frank with the other.

***

The following day Madison wears a minimal disguise of a baseball cap and sunglasses. She also wears jeans and boots with high, wide heels. John doesn't say anything, but knows that those shoes ain't walking shoes. Nevertheless, they walk through Central Park on their way to New York's famous museums. Madison soaks up the thrilling feel of the city. She never imagined, stepping out of the limo for a moment, could be so satisfying. As they approach a road running through the park, John, instinctively, reaches for Madison's hand. He holds onto her tight as they cross the street. Madison appreciates the unexpected, sweet gesture.

***

They hit the Museum of Natural History. It's

filled with huge, dinosaur bones, pyramids, statues and other re-creations of the past. As Madison has been home schooled since the age of nine, textbooks were scarce. In fact, homework was a rarity. Every once in a while, a woman would come and check on her progress, and every once in awhile, Madison would have to act like she did the work.

In actuality Angie took care of it. She created a mountain of schoolwork to show when the government education people came to check up on Madison's progress. If the official got suspicious and started asking too many questions, Angie reached into her deep purse and paid them off. A "good" education cost money.

**

At the Statue of Liberty, Madison feels like a little girl. It's as if she's learning about the world for the first time. For a moment, she steps back and does something she has never done before in her life. She focuses on the moment. She looks at John and thinks about how smart, handsome, and charming he is. She feels the cool breeze coming off the Hudson River, and looks at the big city from the huge monument.

John looks back at her with a smile, as if he knows exactly what she's doing. That's when three young girls approach them. The girls ask Madison that ever so familiar question, "Can we have your autograph?"

Madison obliges.

A mom asks if Madison will take a picture with the girls. Madison does it. She even takes off the cap and sunglasses. But as the picture snaps, other young girls squeeze in and John is squeezed out.

***

It's a perfectly clear day so the Empire State Building offers a breathtaking view which Madison enjoys until another group of young fans ask for a photograph with her. She used to love the attention, now all she wants is to be able to focus on John. But she can't dismiss her fans. It's all part of being Madison Park. John stands to the side as they set up for the photo. Just before the stranger snaps the photo, Madison grabs John and pulls him into the picture. He smiles for the camera.

***

As they walk along the Hudson River on the west side of Manhattan, Madison starts to lag behind. It's just her nature to be fashionable over comfortable. (John lives by the exact opposite rule).

"Slow down my feet are killing me," Madison

whines. "Can't we take a taxicab?"

"Absolutely not, I hate taxies. Were you one of those kids that were in a stroller until the age of ten?"

"I was walking in heels at four years-old!"

John is not impressed.

Madison sits on a bench refusing to budge.

"What are you doing?"

"I need to rest," she says.

Deciding to help the situation, John sits next to her. "Give me your foot."

Madison hesitantly puts her foot on his lap. The truth is, he's dying to get her foot in his hand. He takes the ridiculously large boot off and massages her foot, thinking the whole time how perfect her feet are. He's never had a foot fetish, but her foot is so perfect, he just might develop one.

As he rubs Madison exhales with pleasure. This is the first foot massage she's ever received. And for a girl who spends every waking moment in heels, this is a huge discovery. She can't help but think, "This guy is perfect."

John figures such an exquisite foot has to have something wrong with it, so he lifts it to his nose and takes a whiff. It doesn't smell.

"What are you doing?" Madison asks.

"What?" John, honestly, doesn't see the peculiarity in what he did.

"You just smelled my foot?"

"Is that weird?" John asks.

"I would say that qualifies as weird, yeah!"

"I never said I wasn't a little weird."

"You never said you were."

John is hesitant to tell her that it was such a perfect foot; he wanted to know if it smelled.

"You can rub them all you want, but please, no sniffing!"

John smiles, takes her other boot off and rubs her other foot for awhile.

Madison tilts her head back and sighs. She never new such a simple pleasure could have so much power over her. She could stay in that spot forever.

Eventually, John feels he alleviated enough of the aching so he gently moves Madison's legs off his lap.

"That was great! Thanks," Madison says with a sweet smile.

John picks up her boots, walks calmly to the water's edge and tosses them in the Hudson River. "On we go," he says.

"What did you do that for? Are you crazy?

106

Those were fifteen hundred dollar boots."

"What? My car cost less than that." He doesn't own a car but he made his point. "The only way I would pay fifteen hundred bucks for shoes is if they had rockets on the bottom that propelled me through the air like Lebron James. You can't even walk in those things."

"They're not made for walking."

"Who wears shoes that aren't made for walking?"

"I do! What am I gonna do now?"

John walks over to her, lifts her off the bench and hoists her onto his shoulder.

Madison hangs onto his back, upside down and says, "This is a familiar view. What are you doing?"

John heads off, carrying her.

***

After an hour of Madison wrestling over just the right footwear to go with her outfit, they emerge from "Sneaker Town." On the sidewalk, Madison bends at the knee, and then goes on her tippy toes, feeling out the sneakers. "These things are awesome."

"You've never worn sneakers?"

"Not since I was nine. I forgot how comfortable they are."

107

The huge store window seems to act as a large magnet – the people inside the store are clamoring to get a look at Madison. She doesn't notice, but John does, "Let's go," he says impatiently, as he grabs her hand.

"Where are we going now?"

"Let's lay low for awhile," John says. "I know just the place."

***

It's a beautiful, starry night as every cluster in the sky is amazingly clear. It's truly a wondrous sight. Except it's three o'clock in the afternoon. They're staring at the roof of the Hayden Planetarium. John points out the different constellations as Madison snuggles up to him, burying her face in his chest.

***

Madison and John ride the elevated, subway train through the streets of Brooklyn. Madison eats popcorn as she gazes from the train, car window. It doesn't get more interesting than the sights of Brooklyn.

"Don't fill up on popcorn," John says. "You're getting a gourmet meal."

***

The best place in New York to eat is Grey's

Papaya. John isn't the only one who thinks so. The landmark, hot dog stand is packed with everyone, from native New Yorkers to tourists. John brings over four hot dogs.

"What are you gonna eat?" Madison quips. She can't wait to bite into one. She picks up one with mustard and cheese and chows down. A look of ecstasy appears on her face. With a mouthful, she says, "Angie would kill me if she knew I was eating a hot dog."

***

John and Madison are now doing exactly what nobody should do after eating hot dogs. They're running. A bunch of Madison's fans are chasing them and they're catching up. That's okay because John has a plan. Since the day is almost over he decides he's gonna take Madison on the Staten Island Ferry for the "magic hour." The "magic hour" is a term used by Hollywood moviemakers to describe the hour that the sun goes down. It's the short span of time when the world is aglow with a beautiful, golden hue.

The ferry to Staten Island is literally the only free ride in New York City. As they approach the terminal, John notices the huge, sliding door closing. His eyes get big as he grabs Madison's hand and picks up the pace. The space between the huge door and the

109

jamb is shrinking rapidly. They speed up and with just a foot or two opening they squeeze through, as the door slams closed, shutting out the fans.

They board the large boat. As the sun goes down, the cool, autumn wind whips through Madison's hair.

While they gaze at the sunset, John tells her why he loves New York. "Before I became a firefighter I worked in the city – a desk job. I hated it. But every day on the way to work, I got to see the sun rise. And every day on the way home, I got to see the sunset over the greatest city in the world. It wasn't so bad."

"Are you a Pisces?"

"Ten-four."

"I knew it; I could tell."

"And you, little miss ambitious, must be an Aries."

"April third," Madison confirms.

From inside the huge boat, music plays. It's a lone man at a keyboard. Madison grabs John by the hand and rushes over, dragging him with her. The man finishes his song, as someone drops a dollar in the box next to him.

"Can we play a song?" Madison boldly asks the man.

"Wait a second," John says. "What do you mean we?"

"I mean you and me."

"Nobody asked me," John says.

"Please, do a song with me," Madison pleads, rubbing John's arm.

She's very hard to say no to when she wants something. John throws a big tip in the box and the guy gladly steps aside. "Fine, but I pick the song," John says. He doesn't ask her if the song is okay. He plays "Just My Imagination" by the Temptations.

Madison surprises John – she knows the song well. She sings the song perfectly, as John plays the keyboard. Although originally written from a man's point of view, Madison takes the liberty of singing it from hers. The song tells the tale of a woman watching from her window as the man of her dreams slowly passes by. The few moments stretch into a short eternity, as she wonders what their life would be like together as she sings. *"So we'll be married and raise a family. Have a cozy, little home in the country with two children, maybe three. Out of all the boys in the world, he belongs to me. But it was just my imagination running away with me."*

As the song goes on, a crowd gathers. The man

who was originally at the keyboard joins in for the chorus. His voice is very powerful and is an excellent complement to Madison. At the end of the song, the small crowd applauds. The sun sets behind them.

***

It's a rare quiet night in Manhattan. Traffic doesn't seem heavy or loud. Nobody seems to be in a rush. A dog walker, surrounded by six dogs, casually strolls past, as John drops Madison off at the hotel. It's a long goodbye, as they laugh about the events of the day.

"Would you be interested in a home cooked meal?" John asks.

"You cook too?" Madison says, amazed by the depth of this guy.

"I'm a terrible cook," John confesses. "The guys at the firehouse won't let me near the oven, except to clean it. But my mother can cook."

"A home cooked meal. I would love that."

"And my little sister would love to meet you." John smiles for a moment, but the smile goes away as he gazes into Madison's bright, blue eyes. He carefully pulls her into him, closes his eyes and leans in. He wants to put an exclamation point on the day in the form of a seductive kiss.

Madison is not gonna let him go until she gets that kiss. She squeezes him tight against her.

Suddenly, the doorman rushes outside and obnoxiously clears his throat, killing the moment.

"Leave us alone," Madison says to the doorman.

But the doorman was paid off by Angie to break the two up.

Madison decides that if the doorman wants to watch, that's fine with her. She's gonna get hers either way. She grabs John by the chest, pulls him close and they kiss. She doesn't just want his lips; she's determined to feel every part of his body against hers – every part.

The doorman clears his throat again, but they ignore him, and eventually he turns away, embarrassed.

Madison's internal temperature skyrockets. It's been awhile since she's felt true physical longing. She's suddenly afraid she might drag him up to her hotel room and attack him. She manages to control herself – for now.

***

Madison floats on a cloud as she enters the hotel room where Angie is waiting for her. Despite her good mood, Madison wants to give her some attitude about the doorman. But, once again, Angie

113

out-bitches her. "Where the hell have you been?" She screams.

"It's none of your business."

"You had appearances today."

"I cancelled them," Madison says.

"I do the canceling around here!"

"You wouldn't have done it."

The argument quickly escalates.

"Of course I wouldn't have done it," Angie says. "I have a career to think about."

"I have a life to think about," Madison says.

"Your career is your life."

"No, my career is *your* life," Madison snaps. "It's only part of mine."

"You want everything," Angie replies.

"You never had a problem with that before."

The argument peaks as the two actually seem to be listening to each other – sort of.

"You're losing sight of the goal," Angie barks, as she lights a cigarette.

"Tell me Angie, what is the goal? When does it end? When can I be a woman?"

Angie has no answer for her. She heads out to the balcony to smoke.

Madison goes into the bedroom.

The truth is Angie doesn't want her to be a woman yet. She knows that when that happens, she won't be able to control her.

7

When Does Romance
Become Love?

A taxicab pulls up to a modest, well-maintained, semi-attached, Staten Island home. Madison gets out, approaches the door and knocks. The cab waits.

John comes to the door with his little sister, Krissy – an adorable but feisty, eight year old, Madison Park fan. When Krissy sees her pop idol face to face, she freezes. Her eyes practically pop out of her head.

"Where's the limo?" John asks.

"It wasn't an option," Madison explains. "There were paparazzi everywhere just waiting for the limo to move. So I snuck out the back door and hailed a cab. What a rush!"

"How much is a cab from Midtown Manhattan?" John asks, curious.

"Only seventy-five dollars," Madison boasts.

"Is that all?" John says, sarcastically.

Not picking up on the sarcasm, Madison

responds, "I was surprised too."

John waves her in. Madison is excited to meet the family, but before she can, she tells him, "Actually, I need a little help paying for the cab."

"How much do you need?"

"Seventy-five dollars," Madison says, sheepishly. "Plus tip, of course. I don't carry money. Angie has all of that stuff."

"Stuff?" John heads over to the taxi hoping the cabby takes Visa.

Madison bends down to get eye level with Krissy and says, "You must be the girl with two beautiful, first names."

"Krissy Kelly, it's nice to meet you," she says, holding out her hand.

"I've heard a lot about you."

"Then we're even because I know everything about you." Krissy grabs Madison by the hand and pulls her into the living room.

***

At dinner that night, Madison learns all about John's family. John's father is a retired firefighter. He's laid back and has a strange sense of humor. John's mom is a sweet housewife. John and Madison sit side by side across from Krissy, and John's younger brother

117

by two years, Brian.

John is getting frustrated with his brother's staring.

"You brought Madison Park home for dinner," Brian says, star-struck.

"Brian has a tight grip on the obvious," John says to Madison.

"How am I gonna top that?" Brian adds.

"I'm pretty good friends with Miley Cyrus," Madison says. "Next time I see her, I'll put in a good word for you."

"How about Shakira?" Brian responds, upping the ante.

"Apparently, you like older women," Madison says. "I'll see what I can do."

Brian smiles big in anticipation of what will probably never happen.

John's mom is quiet – too quiet. As sweet as she is, she's suspicious. She doesn't doubt Madison has a good heart. She always thinks the best of people before assuming the worst. But she knows Madison has the potential to be a spoiled, immature princess. Although her real concern is that Madison may hurt her son. She wants to know that her son's heart is more important to Madison than her career. And despite being a

118

positive person she's not sure if that's the case.

John's mom starts with what appears to be an innocent question, "How long are you in New York?"

"I have a concert to make up at the end of the week," Madison answers. "Then I have to finish the tour."

"Then what?"

"My new album drops and I go back on tour."

John's dad interjects, "New York must be like a different planet compared to Oklahoma."

"The Yankee boys are just as sweet," Madison says, as she glances at John.

"She's talking about you," Krissy says to John.

"Thanks Krissy," John says with a chuckle.

"I haven't had a home cooked meal in years. Everything is delicious," Madison says, as she shovels food in her mouth.

Krissy jumps from the table. "Can we play 'Charades' after dinner?"

"Maybe, honey," John's mom answers. She turns to Madison, "Do you play Charades, Madison?"

Madison has her mouth full so she just nods her head yes. But as she nods, a piece of food gets lodged in her throat.

"Mom, Please don't force any embarrassing

games on her," John begs her.

Suddenly Madison starts waving her arms in an attempt to get John's attention.

John's mom notices and smiles, thinking she's playing charades at the dinner table. "I don't think she's embarrassed. We should wait until after dinner, but what the heck."

John's dad sees Madison flail her arms and yells, "It's a movie?"

"How do you know?" Brian asks.

John's dad does the hand signal for movie and says, "She went like this."

Madison realizes nobody is catching on to the fact that she's choking so her eyes begin to bulge from her head.

"Eyes Wide Shut," John's mom guesses.

"The Hills Have Eyes," Brian shouts.

"Spell it out," John's dad says, asking for a little help. "What are the syllables?"

Madison grabs her chest and John's mom ventures another guess, "Untamed Heart?"

Desperate, Madison stands and Brian yells out, "Stand And Deliver."

Madison can't believe this is happening as she starts to pound her own chest in a feeble attempt to

120

dislodge the pot roast.

"King Kong," John's dad shouts.

John is dumbfounded by the game at the dinner table. This is not what he had envisioned.

Madison puts her hands to her throat, which is the universal sign for choking. But they don't respond to it. Apparently, not everyone knows the universal sign for choking.

But John's dad recognizes the choking sign except he assumes she's playing the game so he takes a stab, "The Big Choke."

"It's The Big Chill, dad," Brian says, correcting him.

Just before Madison turns blue, Krissy realizes what's happening and shouts, "Oh my God, she's choking."

John leaps to his feet and spins Madison around. Her back is to him as he puts his arms around her seizing her in a bear hug. Performing the Heimlich maneuver, he squeezes once, twice and the third time – as they say – is a charm. The food flies from her mouth and across the room.

Madison catches her breath and says, "I want Krissy on my team."

Relieved Madison is okay, they all laugh.

Later on that night the real game of Charades kicks into high gear. The whole family is involved, as John, Madison and Krissy are a team against John's mom, dad and brother, Brian. It's John's turn to get up and make a fool of himself. He pulls a small piece of paper from a hat, reads it to himself and cups his mouth with his hands.

"A song, my specialty," Madison says, perking up.

John holds up two fingers and Krissy shouts, "Two words."

Suddenly John breaks out into the robot dance to everyone's shock and awe. The answer is obvious but nobody's guessing. After a few minutes of doing the weirdest, robotic dance ever done in this particular galaxy, John stops and breaks the rules saying, "I know you know what it is."

"Mister Roboto," Madison says confidently. "But I was having too much fun watching you do whatever it was you were doing."

"I was robot dancing and I was good." Still dancing, he boasts, "In fact, I should've been a professional dancer."

"I like the way you dance," Madison says sweetly. "But I wouldn't quit your day job if I were

122

you."

"I have no intention to." The statement seems to take on more meaning than was originally intended.

"That was the worst robot dance I ever saw," Brian snaps.

"Who do you think you are, Justin Timberlake?" John snaps back.

"My hips swivel like – something that swivels real smoothly," Brian says, glaring at Madison.

"I hope it's smoother than your rap," John says.

"Watch this." Brian starts dancing all crazy like.

John starts dancing even weirder.

It's a crazy, robot, dance battle.

John's mom puts on some music.

Madison thinks, "They must know how odd they look."

John's mom and dad sit on the couch and cheer them on, until mom pulls dad off the couch and they join in.

Then the boys pull Krissy into the wacky dance party. Krissy jumps around like a robotic kangaroo on Red Bull and suddenly it dawns on Madison. This show isn't for her; it's for Krissy. The huge display of silliness is simply to make their little sister laugh. Madison is so touched she wants to be a part of it. She busts out her own silly, robot dance. Krissy laughs her head off, without missing a step. In just a few hours Madison feels like part of a family – a real family. As happy as Madison is at this moment, she can't help but think about the kind of family fun she missed out on, during her childhood.

The wacky, dance party ends when Krissy plops on the couch – exhausted. The music stops and the adults sit down too. John's mom interjects an idea, "John, play something on the piano for us."

"I don't think so," John says.

"What a great idea," Madison says sarcastically; knowing John doesn't want to be the center of attention.

"You can sing along, Madison," John's mom says, surprising Madison.

John smiles, as Madison has now been pulled into the web. He turns to Madison and in a mock-tone says, "Yeah Madison, you can sing."

Madison's not about to argue with John's mom, so she grabs John's hand and pulls him up off the couch. The two head to the small piano and sit on the small bench.

"Play 'Rotten Love'," Krissy shouts.

It happens to be one of Madison's hit songs.

Madison doesn't feel the song is appropriate for the situation. But before she can suggest something else John says, "I wrote words to that melody that I played for you on our first date. Do you wanna give it a go?"

"Sure," she says excitedly.

John pulls a folded piece of paper from his pocket. Madison unfolds the paper and scans the lyrics. "Okay, I'm ready."

John plays the music as she sings. The first chorus is a little rough, because she doesn't know it, but she quickly catches on to the poetry of the words. It tells the tale of a simple boy who meets an exciting girl who turns his world upside down and makes him feel things he's never felt before. You don't have to be a brain surgeon to figure out who the song is about. She's singing a song about herself.

When they're done, the family applauds.

John looks at Madison, mesmerized by her talent and beauty.

Madison gazes into his eyes as if he gave her the sweetest gift anyone has ever given her – a song.

Later that night Madison puts Krissy to bed.

"No one in my class is gonna believe Madison Park tucked me into bed," Krissy says.

"That doesn't mean you shouldn't tell them," Madison says.

"You bet your butt I'm gonna tell them."

"Sleep tight; don't let the bed bugs bite," Madison says, tucking her in.

"Bed bugs? What bed bugs?" Krissy freaks. "There are bugs in my bed? And they bite?"

"No, no, I didn't mean it literally," Madison says.

"They're gonna eat me in my sleep, aren't they?" Krissy says with fear in her eyes.

"Forget I said that. There's no such thing as bed bugs. I made the whole thing up."

Suddenly Krissy laughs hysterically. Between laughs she manages to say, "I totally got you."

Madison can't believe the little girl was messing with her, but instead of being annoyed she smiles. Krissy's uncontrolled laugh is a powerful one for a young girl and it's absolutely infectious. Madison finds herself naturally laughing along with Krissy. To exact revenge – and to keep the laughter going – she tickles Krissy.

From outside the bedroom door, John peeks in watching the tickle fight. He feels he's getting a revealing glimpse of the simple, Midwestern girl inside the international pop star. He wonders to himself; can this be real? Can she be this great? Can this really work?

The night ends as John walks Madison to the waiting cab. John and Madison face each other, and John says, "I'm glad you came."

"Me too, I absolutely love your family. Do you think they would adopt me?" Madison asks.

"I don't know but I'll put in a good word for you."

"Thanks," Madison says. Suddenly, she has a solemn look on her face, "Before my dad died, my parents fought because he wanted more kids, and Angie didn't. I took Angie's side, because I didn't want to share him. I was so selfish. So stupid."

John gazes into her eyes and says, "But if you had a brother or sister then that would be another little boy or girl that grew up without the greatest dad in the world."

Madison is so touched by the comment; it brings a tear to her eye. "I'm jealous of your family. Is that weird?"

John looks back at his house and spies his wacky family, clamoring at the window, for a view of the goodnight kiss. "Jealous of them? Yeah, that's weird."

Madison smiles and leans in for a kiss. Suddenly a group of young girls, dressed in pajamas, come running around the corner armed with pen and paper.

Startled by the mob of young girls, John pulls away from the embrace and tells Madison, "Get in the car."

Madison is disappointed and frustrated. She doesn't want to let go of him. But he gives her a quick peck on the lips and practically shoves her in the cab.

But Madison puts her foot down. She comes back out of the cab for another kiss. She grabs John and pulls him in close, pressing her lips against his. This kiss lasts a lot longer than the first one.

By now the mob has reached the cab but John and Madison are still embraced in the long, wet kiss.

The young girls giggle.

Madison puts her hand up to signal the kids to stop and they do. They're young and excited to meet their idol but they're smart enough to know not to disturb a moment like this. They wait patiently.

Finally Madison and John pry themselves apart. Madison grabs one of the young girl's pens and with a big smile signs autographs.

John smiles just as big until one of the little girls' looks at him and says, "That's not Jorden."

***

Later that night, back at the hotel, Madison floats through the halls stuck in some weird, wonderful, dreamlike state. When she reaches the door to her hotel room the feelings overwhelm her as she takes a Hollywood moment. She leans back against the door, closes her eyes and imagines herself back in the firefighter's embrace. His lips pressed against her lips, his muscular chest pressed against her breasts, his chiseled stomach pressed against her belly, his arms squeezing her tight. The strength of his embrace sends chills down her spine while at the same time her temperature soars.

To bring herself back she breathes deep, composes herself, faces the door and enters her hotel room.

Inside the hotel room, Madison is confronted with an invasion of red and white roses. The room is lined from wall to wall. She immediately feels the rush of feelings overtake her again. John's gesture nearly brings tears to her eyes, as she can only imagine how much this must have cost. A humble, blue-collar guy could blow a whole paycheck to fill that room with roses. It seems there's nothing he wouldn't do for her. Of course he did risk his life for her, so that should

129

have been obvious.

She leans over, closes her eyes, and puts her face to one of the flowers. She breathes in deep as if she's taking in much more than the simple, beautiful, aroma. She says out loud to herself, "This must have cost a fortune."

"You're worth it," a voice says.

Madison looks up – startled.

He steps out from behind the wall of roses.

"Jorden!" She says.

"Surprise."

"You did this?" She asks, trying not to show her disappointment.

"Who else?"

"What are you doing here?" Madison asks, as she stands across the room awkwardly – her arms folded. "I mean, what about the tour?"

"I left the tour to be with you," Jorden says.

"But that's crazy; you've worked so hard."

"Is it crazy? You are the most important thing in my life. It may have taken me awhile to figure that out, but I know it now. I don't want to be apart anymore. I'm here to stay."

8
Will I What?

Back at the firehouse John does something he should have done a long time ago. He takes down the picture of his ex-girlfriend, Melissa, from his locker door. In its place, he puts a picture of him and Madison and a bunch of her young fans at the Empire State Building. He puts on his uniform, closes his locker and heads into the kitchen.

Frank and I gaze at the television as we prepare lunch. John immediately picks up on our frozen stares as he walks in, so he turns to the T.V.

On the screen, Cynthia Santana reports, "Today in New York; just a day after Madison Park was spotted all over the city with her rescuer, John Kelly. She and Jorden Vanderpool held a press conference announcing that Jorden is leaving the 'All Grown Up Tour' and will be joining Madison for a special concert in New York."

One clip on the television has Jorden and Madison walking down the street holding hands. Another clip shows them talking to reporters at the concert hall during a rehearsal.

"Madison and Jorden will be hard at work preparing for the duet they're performing together. On a more personal note, Jorden squashed any rumors about their relationship, saying, 'They're solid as a rock'."

The television abruptly goes to commercial and John asks, "Who the hell is Jorden Vanderpool?"

"Are you kidding?" I ask, wondering if John lives under a rock. "Don't you read Teen Beat magazine?"

"No, you do?"

"Of course not," I say, back-pedaling. Sometimes I reveal way too much about myself – which can easily be used against me in the firehouse. I really have to learn to think before I speak.

***

Madison is hard at work at the studio, singing her new song about being confused in love. On the other side of the glass, a sound engineer brings the music down. Standing over the engineer, Angie gives her two thumbs up.

The light goes off which indicates recording has stopped and Jorden enters. He leans in to kiss Madison and she turns her head so his lips land on her cheek. It's awkward, but he's not gonna question it. He's getting what he really wants – time in the studio with Madison.

Before they sing the duet, Jorden says, "You were my inspiration for writing this song." Of course, Jorden didn't write it. But that isn't going to stop him from taking credit for it.

He signals to the engineer. As the engineer slides a few knobs up, the music rises.

At first, the awkwardness floats in the room like a thick fog. But as they sing, the emotion of the song, about a couple that struggles to find time and love for each other, draws them closer together. Suddenly the feelings Madison has for Jorden begin working their way to the surface. She realizes how much she's missed him. Their past – so rich with beautiful, innocent memories comes flooding back. They gaze deep into each other's eyes.

On the other side of the glass Steven enters the small, control room and joins Angie. They focus on the rekindling magic between the two pop stars when Madison's iPhone rings. A photo of John in his firefighting gear appears as the words, "My Hero is Calling" scrolls across the bottom of the screen.

Behind the soundproof glass, in the middle of belting the new song, Madison can't hear the phone.

Angie waits for it to stop, picks it up and erases the call log – like it never happened.

Steven notices and it puts a mischievous smirk on his face.

As the song comes to an end the engineer brings the music down.

"I think we have a hit," Steven says to Angie.

She nods, not necessarily agreeing or disagreeing with him.

Inside the booth, Madison, face to face with Jorden, asks him, "You wrote that?"

"Yes, for you," he says.

***

John reads as Frank enters the kitchen of the firehouse. John closes the book abruptly. Frank peers at the book and says, "Ladder Company Operations. I see you're brushing up on your firefighting procedures." He pours himself a cup of coffee.

"You can't know the job too well," John says.

Frank smirks. He's on to him. He approaches him and opens the book revealing "Teen Beat" magazine inside. On the cover of the magazine is a large picture of Madison and Jorden. The caption underneath reads, "The Dynamic Duet Endure."

"Teen Beat magazine isn't gonna help you pass the Lieutenant's test."

"Teen Beat says they're soul mates," John says.

"You can't be worried about what Teen Beat says," Frank responds, trying to reassure him.

"She won't return my phone calls."

"That's the worst kind of rejection," Frank says, not making him feel any better.

"I wasn't thinking of it as rejection. I just figured she's busy with the whole rock star thing."

"Oh yeah, I'm sure that's what it is."

At that moment, I enter the kitchen, catching Frank's last sentence. My curiosity is peaked, "What 'what is'?"

"Nothing," John says, having no interest in bringing me in on the conversation.

I really don't care anyway so I quickly change the subject, "What do you say we go out tonight and hit the bar?"

"No thanks."

"Come on, It's ladies night at 'Hook and Ladder.' This is just what you need."

Frank jumps in, "I can't believe I'm about to say thic, but Billy's right, You should go out and have some fun."

***

Now back to me! There's a lot of downtime in my line of work. If I'm not making Madison look perfect, I'm, pretty much, not doing anything. Alone in the hotel room I have to find ways to pass the time so I pop in a DVD. The music comes on and the "Teen Team" explodes onto the stage. They're barely teenagers as Madison, Jorden and three others dance and sing. They wear trendy, baseball caps and baseball jerseys.

Like the graceful thing of beauty I am, I match the moves of the young, adolescent stars perfectly. It's wrong that I wasn't chosen for that show. I would've been perfect. Okay, I can't sing but that wouldn't stop me. I know every word of the "Teen Team" anthem and I'm a diva as I belt out the lyrics.

Little do I know, about ten feet behind me my life is about to collide in a nuclear explosion of embarrassment. Madison and Jorden enter, catching most of my show. They could warn me that they are there, but I imagine they are having too much fun watching me destroy any respect Maddy might have for me.

Eventually I spin, and as soon as I see them, I run out of the room. But I stick my head back inside, and leave them with, "That's how it's done!"

"What do you want to do tonight?" Madison asks Jorden. Before he can answer, she suggests, "Let's go ice skating at Rockerfeller Center!"

"Why don't I just run down Avenue of the America's screaming, 'I'm Jorden Vanderpool, ruin my night.' I don't want to deal with autograph hounds and paparazzi."

"What are we going to do then, sit around the hotel room all night?"

"You never had a problem with that before."

"It gets old." Madison plops down on the couch.

"You, me, room service and a big screen T.V. That never gets old to me," Jorden says.

"I'm sorry, I guess I'm a little cranky," she says. "I should go to bed and get some sleep. I have a long day in the studio tomorrow." She heads to the bedroom.

"Okay, but if you can't sleep, I'll be right across the hall."

"Ten four," Madison acknowledges, as she closes the bedroom door behind her.

Jorden has a confused look on his face as he says to himself, "Ten four?" Before he retreats to his room he notices a small piece of paper on the counter. He picks it up and reads. It's John's song. He takes it, puts it in his pocket and retreats to his room.

***

John's evening is not quite so quiet. In a dark corner of a loud, crowded bar a young, attractive brunette writes on a coaster and hands it to him. She runs her fingertips along John's forearm in a subtle but revealing way. It seems to be a little too much, too soon, for John.

"Excuse me," he says, as he walks away.

I'm a few feet away hookin' up with a chick but I'm the one who dragged him out so I feel a certain responsibility that he has a good time. I manage to catch the scene between John and the brunette chick. I see

John walk out of the bar so I go after him.

Outside, John heads directly to the corner and looks at the coaster with the seven digits. He's about to toss the coaster in a trashcan when I stop him. "Don't even think about it!"

John freezes.

"Don't you dare. That is an attractive girl in your hand."

"If you like her so much then you take the number."

"Okay." I head toward him to get the phone number then I change my mind, "I can't take it. You earned it, not me."

"Since when do you care who actually got the number?"

"Since now I guess. Despite what you think of me, I have principles."

"You don't know the meaning of the word."

"A comprehensive and fundamental law, doctrine or assumption." I belch to drive home my point.

"I stand corrected," John mumbles under his breath.

I lean on a car and preach, "This is not about me." Then I completely forget what we're talking about.

John waves a hand in my face. "You were saying?"

"What were we talking about?" It comes back to me. "The phone number; put it in your pocket."

"No," John replies sternly.

"Put the number in your pocket."

"No."

"That girl in there is cute and she wants you. Madison Park used you. She had you show her a good time in New York. You're her 'New York Boy Toy.' There's a John Kelly in every city for her. When the gig is up, she goes back to her pop star boyfriend."

"I don't believe that," John says adamantly.

"Why do you think women are so innocent?" I don't give him time to answer since I haven't driven home my point just yet. "They're not innocent; it's all an act. They're guilty as hell! Chicks should do time the way they break hearts. They're criminals of love. If my heart's a casino, they're in and out like Brad Pitt and Matt Damon in 'Ocean's Eleven.' But they ain't stealing money. They're robbing me of my love."

"Now you're not making any sense."

"But what you mean to say is 'I am making sense,' ain't I?" I sit on a parked car and reminisce about lost loves.

"No," John says stubbornly.

"She's finished with you. Move on!"

John thinks about what I'm saying. It's apparent I'm getting through to him.

"It's not gonna end like this," he says. He squeezes the coaster, tosses it in the trash and runs off.

Okay, maybe I'm not getting through to him. "Where are you going?" I yell. "I thought we'd go to the diner. There are always chicks at the diner – and I'm hungry. I want a pizza burger. I can't eat a pizza burger alone."

With John out of sight, I reach into the trash and retrieve the coaster with the phone number.

***

John enters the huge luxury hotel on Park Avenue where Madison is staying. The receptionist, Alyssa, is a young woman who doesn't look old enough to be up so late. When she's fifty, she'll probably look thirty but at twenty-five, she looks like a high school freshman. On top of her unnatural, youthful look, she's a loud-mouth, geeky, boy-band groupie.

John confidently tells Alyssa he has come to see Madison Park, and she, just as confidently, tells him there's nobody by that name staying at the hotel. He tries to explain to her who he is but she doesn't care. She's the first line of defense and as small and awkward as she is, she's gonna stand her ground.

"I know she's here. Just tell her John is downstairs."

"It's one o'clock in the morning," Alyssa says.

"Why should that matter if she's not here?"

Busted, Alyssa just smiles.

"I'll just go up, I know the room." John heads toward the elevators. Alyssa picks up the intercom receiver and announces over the loudspeaker, "Code red in the lobby. I repeat, code red in the lobby. Security to the lobby, forthwith."

As the security guards heed the announcement and hurry to the lobby, John makes a mad dash to the stairwell and bolts up two to three steps at a time. He can hear the rapid footsteps of the guards giving chase.

He thinks to himself, this must be the only place in New York where they don't have old, fat security guards. After twenty flights of steps, John reaches Madison's floor, bursts through the stairwell door, runs down the hallway, turns a corner and smacks into Madison's big bodyguard. John falls backward.

"You wouldn't be trying to get into this room, would you?" The bodyguard asks, looking down at him.

"Actually, that would be the one, yes." John pops up off the floor.

"Well you're going to have to go through me."

"I'm not afraid of you," John says, as he readies himself for attack.

"Then you're not very bright," the bodyguard responds.

John thinks better of challenging the bodyguard – not because he's afraid of him. It would just be too darn time-consuming. John knows the building. The security guards are closing in. He uses his agility to fake him out. He goes left, then right, then left but runs right into the man's chest and falls back again. The narrow halls are not conducive to his strategy.

Plan B it is – John runs right at the huge man and jumps at him in an attempt to knock him over. Instead, the bodyguard catches him in mid air and locks him in a bear hug.

The security guards burst through the stairwell door. The bodyguard hands John over to them and they drag him away.

"Madison, I need to talk to you. Madison!" He

shouts desperately.

The three large, security guards struggle with John. They finally manage to get him into the elevator.

***

What is all that noise? You would think we were at a motel in Cancun during spring break. I get out of bed and open my room door ever so slightly. I know Madison is clueless to the ruckus because she sleeps with earmuffs and a satin blindfold. To say she's a heavy sleeper is an understatement. A nuclear bomb wouldn't wake that girl up. I, on the other hand, am a light sleeper.

I watch the whole scene play out as I have my hotel room door open just enough to get my eyeball through. Desperately, I want to rush out into the hallway and help the modern day Romeo proclaim his love for his one and only Juliet. But I'm a big chicken so that's not an option. I carefully close the door and retreat to the safety of my bed.

***

The security guards finish the job and escort John to the street with a final shove. He walks off in defeat.

Inside the lobby of the hotel, Jorden watches John's humiliation with a proud smile. He saunters over to Alyssa, hands her four concert tickets and says, "As promised, four front row seats."

"I'm not supposed to accept these," Alyssa says. "I was just doing my job."

"Okay," Jorden says, pulling the tickets away.

Alyssa snatches the tickets from his hand, "I won't tell anyone, if you don't. I'm a big fan of yours."

"How big?" Jorden asks with a gross smile on his face.

Alyssa feigns embarrassment, but she's not fooling anyone.

"Want to take a break and come up to my room? I'll order room service," Jorden shamelessly says.

"I'm not hungry," Alyssa says with just as gross of a smile. "And I'd love to come up to your room."

***

What is it this time? I need my beauty sleep. I listen intently and it doesn't take long for me to figure it out. It's that slut, Jorden. He's found another floozy. I can hear them through the wall. I wish I could sleep like Madison. I wouldn't have to listen to those two go at it all night. It sounds like two meerkats fighting over a beetle. At this point it's obvious what I have to do.

***

The following day, I ring the buzzer in anticipation. I've never been inside a real, New York firehouse before. I've had plenty of daydreams about the bunkroom but that's another book. John answers the door and has no idea who I am. How exciting! I

143

introduce myself and put my plan into action. I offer him tickets to Madison's concert and to my surprise he asks, "Her concert with Jorden Vanderpool?"

I didn't think of it like that. He probably isn't crazy about the love of his life gazing deep into another man's eyes. (I use the term "man" loosely when referring to Jorden).

"No thanks," he says.

This is gonna be tougher than I thought. So I go right for the man's jugular. "I didn't take you for a man that would give up so easy." I know he won't like being called a quitter. I just hope he won't beat me up. I'm way too cute to be bruised. Although I look fantastic in blue, but more like baby blue not bruise blue.

"Why shouldn't I give up?" He asks. "She gave up on me."

At this point I want to grab him, shake him and shout, "She didn't give up on you, she didn't give up on you!" But I won't. Instead I tell him very calmly, "You have to trust me."

He gives me a look that shows how vulnerable he really is. I almost fell in love with him right then.

"I'm a New Yorker and New Yorkers know you never trust anyone that says, 'trust me'."

Then he gives me his back. I have never experienced anyone saying no to a Madison Park concert. I'm stumped.

Well, maybe not completely stumped.

I shout, "So you're gonna tell your little sister that you had two tickets to see Madison Park in concert, but because you were too chicken to face Jorden Vanderpool, she isn't gonna see her biggest dream in life come true?"

He stops.

I turn to leave for two reasons. One, I want to add dramatic effect; two, I really thought he was gonna beat me up. I get to the door and grab the doorknob. That's when I hear him say, "Wait."

***

From backstage, I peak through the huge curtain. The concert hall is packed, and Krissy sits on John's shoulders soaking it all up. By the look in her eyes, "a dream come true" might be an understatement. The lights dim and the show starts with an array of laser lights. I love this part. From below, Madison erupts through the stage. She's launched almost fifty feet in the air, attached to invisible wires.

The crowd goes wild.

John is practically consumed by the frenzied

145

teens – swallowed up in adolescent chaos. There are two things about Madison that John notices immediately. I know what you're thinking and no it's not those. The first thing John notices is the first thing Krissy notices. Despite her extensive wardrobe, Madison wears blue jeans and a Ladder Thirty-Nine t-shirt cut off just above her belly button. Normally I would never let her go on stage in a t-shirt but this is different.

Besides, Maddy has turned a corner. She's gonna do what she wants to do and nothing is gonna stand in her way. Maybe she wants to anger Angie – honestly I don't know. But wearing sneakers and a t-shirt – especially that t-shirt – was purposeful.

Excited, Krissy bends forward from John's shoulders until she's face to face with him. She's upside down as she shouts, "She's wearing a Thirty-Nine truck t-shirt."

As Madison rocks on, John is more impressed than he expected to be. He can't help but get into it a little, especially with his little sister mimicking every one of the teen idol's dance moves on his head. Krissy's enjoyment is infectious as John smiles broadly.

Madison sings a song full of sexual innuendo. As she sings, Madison finds John in the crowd. She

146

seductively looks deep into his eyes as she runs her fingers along her exposed mid-section.

As John attempts to make sense of the downright, pornographic stare, he tries to cover Krissy's ears. But her flailing arms knock his hands off. John dismisses the look, knowing she's performing, thinking that's just what she does. Then, suddenly, it hits him; he thinks the whole thing was a performance.

By now I've taken my usual spot at the side of the stage, not far from Jorden, who readies himself to go on. He is a consummate professional. He may not have the most talent in the world but he works hard. And he's been doing it since he was ten so he better be good. The truth is, I'm jealous as I know they're gonna blow the crowd away. I've heard this new song and he and Madison will have the crowd in the palm of their hands. They look great on the cover of the latest tabloid and in a perfect world they would be the perfect couple. But this world is far from perfect.

As he gets his game face on he turns to me and nonchalantly says, "I see the fireman got good seats," as if he's well aware of my diabolical plan. How did he know?

"I don't know what you're talking about," I say, playing dumb.

Jorden smiles that wicked, adulterer-but-kinda-cute smile and spews some serious jealousy when he calmly proclaims, "For your information, no blue collar, white trash, civil service worker is gonna take my girl."

I'm stunned by the comment and I want to shout, "If you care so much about Madison, then what was the deal with the all night 'sexcapade' with the nerdy – but awkwardly sexy – hotel receptionist?" But for the first time in my life I bite my lip. Madison's heart is too important to me so I can't reveal my hand just yet. If he knows the potential reputation-damaging information I hold in my head, then he has the upper hand. I have to be cool.

With every drop of strength I have, I stand there like a statue and ignore him. The music fades and rises again, and Jorden runs on to the stage. I'm off the hook.

The song starts out upbeat and powerful. Madison and Jorden take turns singing one verse each until they sing the chorus together and the crowd gets into it – swaying back and forth.

John has a look on his face like he's about to puke.

Opposite the stage Steven Stanton and Angie look on as the duet captivates the young audience.

"The kids really love this song," Steven boasts, proud of himself.

Angie nods her head up and down somewhat reluctant to agree. But it's obvious by the roar of the crowd.

"I heard Madison's new album and there's a couple of potential hits, but none that's going to be as big as this one," Steven adds.

"That's your opinion," Angie responds.

In the midst of the chorus the crowd roars.

"Apparently, it's their opinion too," Steven says with an arrogant smirk.

Angie ignores him.

"Angie, I'm willing to hand over the song for a small percentage. Put the duet on Madison's new album, and we'll take fifteen percent of sales."

"As opposed to putting it on Jorden's album," she says sarcastically.

"We both know Jorden's not putting out a solo album anytime soon," Steven says. "If he has a future as a solo artist, he has to get this song out on Madison's album. We need you Angie, if that's what I have to say. We need Madison. Now do we have a deal?"

"Five percent," Angie says sternly.

149

"Ten." Steven says reluctantly.

"Five." Angie says, not budging.

Steven is frustrated. He knows she's not gonna budge from five percent and he's not one to waste his breath so he changes the deal. "Fine, five percent, but Jorden sings the duet with her on the new tour and he opens for her."

"I already have opening acts."

"This song is the difference between the album going gold and the album going platinum. Besides, if Jorden is on tour with her, she won't be running around town with the local 'yahoos'."

"Watch your mouth. That's my daughter."

But Angie knows he has a point. She hates to feel like she's falling into his trap but she wants to do the best thing for her daughter. Between the extra royalties the album will make with the duet, in addition to the publicity a romantic reunion with Jorden will create, she has no choice. She nods and says, "Okay, draw up the papers."

Steven flashes a repugnant, victory grin.

The song finally ends with a seemingly magical moment between the two pop stars, as they seem to hold the same note for an eternity.

The crowd roars.

John exhales a big sigh of relief. He's glad it's over.

But the nightmare has only just begun. It seems Jorden has something up his sleeve nobody could have predicted. Even Steven looks on, curious, as Jorden prepares the crowd for an announcement.

By the way, if I knew this was coming before the song began I would have run out on stage and told Madison everything about the nauseating liaison the night before. But even I am shocked as Jorden says to the crowd, "I've been meaning to do this for awhile now." He takes Madison's hand, kneels and proclaims, "Madison Park, you are the beautiful oceans and the endless, green pastures of my earth. You are the magical clouds and shining stars in my sky. You're always the silver lining when stormy clouds loom overhead. What I'm saying is; 'I'm head over heels in love with you'."

Jorden whips out a huge ring. It's so big; he must have sold all three of his humvee's to pay for it. The crowd of young girls reacts wildly as if he's proposing to each and every one of them.

Despite the momentary roar, they quickly hush so they can hear the imminent proposal.

Then he does it.

"Madison Park, will you marry me?"

Again the crowd roars.

John and Krissy are stunned. They are the only two in the crowd not cheering, besides me. Again the crowd hushes like it's some kind of weird dance, as they anticipate Madison's proclamation of: I'd love to marry you.

But Madison hesitates and instinctively looks to John in the crowd. She thinks she's the only one that knows who she's looking for and what's going on in her head. But I know. And Jorden knows. And Angie sees her glance at the firefighter. It's as if she's begging him to rescue her from this awkward and unexpected situation.

There's little John can do, and Madison is on the spot. She just blurts out, "How can I say no?"

"I'll take that as a yes," Jorden says.

(Even though it isn't one — as far as I'm concerned.) From the side of the stage, I nearly break down in tears when I see the look on John's face. He looked like the heel just broke off his favorite pair of Salvatore Ferragamo shoes.

The crowd, once again, goes wild as Jorden slips the ring on Madison's finger. He's not finished, though. Suddenly, a lone piano player at the corner of the stage begins to play a song.

"Everyone should have some nice 'Bling'," Jorden proclaims to the crowd. "But our love is not defined by a piece of jewelry – no matter how big and expensive it might be. But maybe I can give you just a small idea of how much I care about this girl. Madison, this is my gift to you."

If you're as smart as I think you are then I don't have to tell you what song it is. That's right, Jorden sings John's song to Madison.

Right now there's a fire roaring inside of John.

Krissy bends over and shouts in his face, "Johnny, that's your song!" She picks her head up and shouts, "Jorden Vanderpool is a butthole!"

When the song ends and the curtain falls, Madison storms off stage, past me, and into her dressing room.

Jorden strolls in behind her.

I'm right behind him. I sit in the corner hoping she won't realize I'm there.

"Quentin, would you excuse us?" She says.

"Don't mind me, I won't interrupt."

She stares at me until I retreat, "Fine, I'll be right outside the door if you need me." I'm not kidding, either. I hear every word through the thin door.

The first thing she does is ask him, "How could you put me on the spot like that?"

"What are you talking about? I want to spend the rest of my life with you," Jorden says.

"I haven't seen you in months. I almost die in a fire and you show up a week later after I already fell in love with someone else."

"What?" Jorden asks shocked, as I rejoice on the other side of the door.

"In the years that we have known each other, you have never written me a song."

"I wrote the duet."

"Your manager wrote the duet."

Jorden pretends to be offended but is really wondering about how she found out.

Okay, I might have overheard Jorden and Steven talking. And I might have mentioned it to Madison. Okay, I did. I am diabolically brilliant!

"That was his song for me – from him," Madison explains. "How can I ever forgive you for what you just did?" She turns and says to herself, "And will he ever forgive me?"

She gives him back the ring.

***

On the subway train back to the firehouse John

apologizes to Krissy, "I'm sorry we didn't go backstage. I know you would have liked to see Madison."

"No big deal, I already met her. Been there, done that," Krissy says. "Anyway, I understand."

"You do huh?" John says with a chuckle, thinking she couldn't possibly understand.

"I see the way she looks at you."

"Oh really, and how is that?" John asks with a smirk.

"Like you're a piece of meat and she's a hungry lioness."

"What?"

"I think you know what I mean," she confidently adds.

"No more Discovery Channel for you."

9

Whose Bra Is In My Boot?

The following night at the firehouse, John sits alone in the kitchen. The firefighters are all upstairs getting some rest when the doorbell rings. John answers.

It's Madison.

"Can I come in?" She sheepishly asks.

John can't imagine she could have a good explanation for the previous night's events, but he's willing to listen. He lets her inside.

"Did you enjoy the show last night?" She asks.

"Are you serious?"

"Okay, stupid question," she says, as she nervously plays with her hair. "That's why I'm here. He put me on the spot and I panicked. I didn't know what to do."

"How about saying no?" John says bluntly.

"I did – afterward."

"How could you let him sing my song? That was my song for you. That's sacred."

"I'm not good under pressure. I was wrong. What he did was wrong and I told him that. Jorden and I have been together for a long time but our relationship was based on convenience. I don't want convenience anymore. I want passion and romance. I want that funny feeling in my belly every time my guy walks into the room. The feeling I get with you."

"Are saying I make you sick?" John quips.

"Just a little nauseous," she says.

John laughs and Madison leans in for a soft kiss.

A moment later they pull their lips apart and Madison says, "I've never been on a fire truck."

John takes Madison by the hand and leads her from the kitchen to the garage where the truck is parked. He shows her where he keeps his firefighting gear. She decides she's gonna try it on. She jumps in his boots and pulls up the suspenders on the pants over her shoulders. She puts on the bunker coat and helmet. She looks like the most adorable firefighter ever. Only she could make firefighting gear sexy. She picks up the halligan tool that the firefighters use to break open doors at fires. She can barely hold the thirty-pound tool.

John wields it like it's a small screwdriver.

Madison has a big smile on her face as she attempts to walk around the garage with the gear on. She approaches John and says, "I'm ready for action."

"So am I," John says. But he isn't talking about the same thing. He leans in for a soft kiss.

She kisses back, caressing the back of his head with her hand.

Maybe they are talking about the same thing.

***

I hate "Texas Hold 'em." I always go "all in" too soon and end up a spectator the rest of the game. But tonight I'm gonna go downstairs, sit on the fire truck and

157

listen to the department radio. If there's a fire somewhere in the city I'll be able hear all the transmissions. It can be pretty entertaining and it'll give me something to do. What happens next will stay with me for quite some time. I quietly open the door on the way to the garage. That's when I see John kissing another firefighter. I'm frozen for a second but, somehow, I manage to retreat in my catatonic state of shock. I don't believe it – he always seemed so "not gay." I'm devastated. I've taken showers with him. Let me clarify that; not *with* him but at the same time. You know what I mean.

I turn and retreat back through the same door. In the kitchen, I catch my breath and try to make sense of the situation. I'll admit I've kissed a man passionately once, yes that's true. But little did I know it was "he-ladies" night at "Limelight" and he had great boobs. I never noticed the Adam's Apple. It's not the same thing.

***

John and Madison never knew Billy was there.

John takes the helmet off her head. His lips never leave hers as he slowly unhooks the bunker coat. He rolls the suspenders off of her shoulders, sliding the bunker pants down. He wraps his arms around her tightly as their lips get warmer and softer and wetter.

In this passionate hug he lifts her right out of the big boots, carries her to the fire truck and climbs on, placing her on the jump seat. They both heat up, as nothing else exists in the world for each of them than the other.

158

As they embrace, Madison digs her face in John's chest. He smells like a man. No cologne, no lavender moisturizer. Just the natural scent of a man – it's intoxicating.

One article of clothing after another flies from the truck window as they take advantage of every inch of the truck's cab.

Locked in a tight embrace, John looks deep into Madison's eyes and says passionately, "I'm falling in. . . *'Bee-Doop'."* The tone alarm blares.

"What?" Madison asks.

But John has no time to repeat himself as the other firefighters race to the truck to answer the call.

John and Madison rush to pick up their clothes.

"What did you say?" Madison asks again, as she fixes herself up.

***

Just then Captain Jack and Frank slide the pole and get to the truck. I run in and immediately notice Madison and her disheveled, look and think, "Damn, I'm jealous – and relieved John isn't gay."

"Excuse us, I hope we didn't interrupt anything," Frank says, suspicious.

John and Madison shake their heads and lie in unison, "No, of course not."

I place my foot into my boot and encounter an obstruction. I pull my foot out, reach in the boot and retrieve a bra. With a smirk on my face, I politely hand Madison the bra. She doesn't seem embarrassed.

"Do you want to come along for a ride?" Captain

159

Jack asks Madison, as John gets his gear on.

"Sure," Madison says, excited.

She jumps on the fire truck and the truck pulls out of quarters.

As the fire truck barrels down the streets of New York the dispatcher comes over the radio, "Manhattan to Ladder Thirty-Nine."

Captain Jack picks up the radio receiver and responds, "Ladder Thirty-Nine."

"We have a confirmed ten seventy-five," the dispatcher says over the radio.

Frank hears the dispatcher and yells to me and John in the back, "We got a job!"

John and I hurriedly get our air masks on and tighten up our gear.

Madison can sense the tension. She suddenly becomes eerily quiet.

Captain Jack reads the response ticket and shouts, "Four story, brownstone building. Billy, take the aerial ladder to the roof."

"Ten four," I respond.

The adrenaline is pumping as John and I rush to get geared up.

Madison is frozen as the sudden intensity and seriousness of the situation hits her.

The fire truck pulls up to a burning building. Fire shoots from three windows, lighting up the neighborhood. I jump out and help Frank set the tormentors for the aerial ladder.

John tells Madison to stay on the truck.

"You're going in there?" Madison asks with terror in her voice. She grabs his arm, as if she can stop him.

"It's my job," he tells her.

"But it's on fire!"

"We'll have to discuss this later," John says.

He heads toward the burning building with Captain Jack. When they reach the front door, John wedges his halligan tool between the door and the jamb and forces the door open.

"I'll go right, you go left," Captain Jack says.

They mask up and crawl in.

On top of the fire truck Frank pushes and pulls the small levers, raising the huge, aerial ladder to the roof of the building. When the ladder rests on the ledge of the building's roof, I quickly climb to the top and hop on the roof.

Inside the fire truck, Madison listens to all the radio transmissions of the firefighters inside the burning building. She hears John's voice over the radio, "Cap, I'm at a locked door with smoke pushing from underneath; I'm gonna force the door open."

She hears Captain Jack acknowledge John's message, "Ten-four."

On the roof of the building, I warn the guys inside, "Heads up below, I'm taking the glass." I take my six-foot hook and thrust it through the skylight, shattering the glass. I duck away from the thick, black smoke and hot gases that are released through the opening.

***

Inside the fire building, John is pinned to the

161

floor by the searing heat until the glass from the skylight crashes down around him. He covers to protect himself. The opening in the roof offers enough relief to allow John to get up off the floor and get back to forcing the door open. When it pops, he crawls inside the room and searches for people. He doesn't find any victims but the intense heat makes it apparent he's found the fire. John stops to transmit a message over his radio, "Cap, I have access to the fire in a second floor bedroom. Primary search is negative."

Suddenly a loud groaning noise is heard as an indication of stress on the building, and from nowhere, the ceiling comes crashing down. Everyone hears the thunderous collapse as the building shakes. When the dust and smoke settle, Captain Jack calls us over the radio to make sure we're alright.

John is the only one that doesn't respond.

"John, are you alright?" Captain Jack asks again, over the radio.

No answer.

He tries again, "Thirty-Nine to Irons; John, answer me."

Once again, he gets no response.

Inside the fire truck, Madison sits with a blank stare, still listening to the transmissions over the truck's radio, "John, where are you?" Captain Jack asks again. Suddenly Madison hears John's voice over the radio, "Mayday, mayday, mayday, I'm trapped. The ceiling came down on me and I'm trapped; mayday, mayday, mayday."

"We're coming to get you, hang tight," Captain Jack responds, from a smoky hallway inside the building.

From the rooftop, I rush to the rear, fire escape, climb down to a window, shatter the glass with my tool and dive in.

In front of the building, Frank moves the ladder from the roof to a window. He climbs up, breaks the glass and squeezes through.

In the truck, Madison, frozen with fear, listens intently. She stares blankly into space as John's voice comes over the radio once again, "Mayday, mayday, mayday." She never imagined she'd hear those dreadful words again. She drifts off to that day when she was nine years old.

***

Young Madison sits patiently, listening to country music, in the patrol car. The gunshots ring out. Then she hears, "Mayday, mayday, mayday," over the police radio. It's her father inside the liquor store. "Mayday, mayday, mayday."

Inside the liquor store, Sheriff Park and the robber lie on the floor bleeding. The robber is hit in the stomach. Sheriff Park took the blast from the shotgun right in the chest.

"Mayday, mayday, mayday," Sheriff Park urgently transmits through his walkie-talkie. "Officer down, one-ten Main Street. I repeat, officer down."

Out front, the getaway car peels away, leaving the robber behind.

The dispatcher responds immediately and sends

all available police units from the surrounding towns and an ambulance. Madison instinctively knows this is bad, but she's terrified and doesn't know what to do. So she does what any scared, little girl would do; she gets out of the car to look for her father. She enters the store through the back door.

At the front of the store, Gabe, blood splashed across his face, sits paralyzed by fear. Madison only walks a few steps into the small store when she sees her father lying on the floor bleeding. He still has his gun trained on the robber who lies on the floor, squirming, about ten feet away.

When Sheriff Park sees Madison, he immediately shouts, "Maddy, get out of here. Run, Maddy, Run!"

Tears roll down her face as she turns and runs out the back door, down the tree-lined street, as other sheriffs from neighboring towns approach. She'll never forget that horrible day. Her father's voice will forever echo in her head, "Mayday, mayday, mayday."

***

Madison suddenly snaps back to the present as this time it's John's frightened voice crackling over the radio, "Mayday, mayday, mayday." Tears roll down her cheeks as she climbs off of the fire truck and heeds her father's last words – "Run, Maddy, run." She runs off as fast as she can.

***

In the fire building, the smoke is getting thicker and blacker. The heat intensifies around John as he struggles to free himself. I finally reach him and try to help. I take his halligan tool and swing it at the heavy timber in order to break it up.

Captain Jack arrives and immediately feels the high heat so he calls for water over the radio, "We need a hose line in this room forthwith." Captain Jack attempts to move the debris as I continue to chop at it to free John.

Finally, the other firefighters arrive with a hose line. They put water on the fire that continues to burn inches away from John. But it's not until Frank arrives that he, Captain Jack and I lift the large piece of plywood ceiling off of John. Frank pulls him out and drags him toward the front exit of the building.

Visibility is zero. It's a long way out, as the three of us have to navigate down the steps and through a long, narrow hallway in thick, black smoke.

The other firefighters with the hose line hold their position as Captain Jack, Frank and I burst into the fresh air, pulling John behind us. He is barely conscious and drags his hurt leg behind him. We all pull our masks off and take a deep breath.

John, on his hands and knees, attempts to catch his breath. He can barely lift his head up toward the fire truck. It's obvious he's looking for Madison, but all he can see is the door she left open when she ran off. Exhaustion overcomes him, as he passes out. Fire laps from one window above him casting an ominous, yellow hue over the fire-ground.

Back at the hotel, the glow of the fireplace reflects on Madison's face, as she sits and ponders. She stares blankly into the fire, sitting rigidly as if her life has been altered forever. There's a knock at the door, but she ignores it. She wants to stay in her own distant world surrounded by her thoughts.

Jorden decides to enter anyway. He takes a seat alongside her. He immediately notices she's not quite right so he asks, "Are you alright?"

"Fine," she lies.

Maybe he's naïve, or maybe he's arrogant, but he thinks she's still upset over the premature, public proposal so he apologizes, "I'm sorry I put you on the spot. I shouldn't have done that. I was desperate. I took our relationship for granted. I screwed up so many times and I was afraid I had lost you forever. I still consider you my best friend. I'm sorry."

Madison continues to stare into the fireplace in some sort of trance. "I always wanted an autumn wedding," she says without turning her head.

"What?" Jorden asks, confused.

"Can't you picture it?" She finally turns. "Flowers as far as the eye can see. Dozens of ice sculptures, cases of champagne, crates of caviar. As I walk down the aisle, rose petals draped in the colors of autumn will fall gently overhead as a live choir sings Pachelbel's Cannon in D. It will be so grand. Ask me again."

"But. . ." Jorden says, stuttering.

"Ask me again."

Jorden is suspicious of her motives but is tempted by the benefits he can reap from a union like this so he kneels and asks, "Madison, will you marry me?"

Madison smiles.

***

I watch John from the doorway of his hospital room. He stares at the television from his bed and flips through the channels so rapidly he couldn't possibly know what he's missing. He finally stops when he sees Cynthia Santana on the screen. Apparently, she's moving up in the world as she proudly announces, "It's official and Hollywood Today is first to break the story. Madison Park has confirmed today that she will wed long time, boyfriend Jorden Vanderpool. And they're not wasting any time. The ceremony will take place at her estate in Oklahoma in two weeks, and only I will be there to cover it. That's right, Hollywood Today obtained exclusive rights to cover the wedding, and I've been chosen to represent. It's hard work but somebody's got to do it."

When she's done John does what any brokenhearted guy would do. He picks up the nearest bouquet of flowers and tosses them at the television.

That's my queue. I enter and joke, "Those were the prettiest ones I could find."

"Billy, just the person I want to see."

"I don't here that often."

John shuts off the television, and swings his legs to the side so he's sitting on the edge of the bed.

"How are you feeling?" I ask.

"Like a ceiling fell on me," John says, as he attempts to dress himself.

"Where do you think you're going?"

"*We* are going to a bar."

"Are you allowed to leave the hospital?"

"No. The concussion and the broken ribs qualified me for an extended stay but I'm thirsty. I need a drink and I need to get a girl off my mind."

"My specialty."

"Tie my shoes," John pleads. "I can't bend over."

As I tie his shoes, I declare, "I just want to go on record as saying, I think this is a bad idea. That being said, I got the first round."

10

A Blast From The Past

John talks to a red-head at a table as I order the beers at the bar. When I return to the table with the beers the girl is gone. I ask, "What was going on over here?"

"Nothing," John says.

"Don't tell me 'nothing.' I could tell from the bar that she was into you."

"Can I have a couple of beers before you have me hooking-up with every girl that walks into the bar?"

"That's a great idea." The proverbial light bulb goes on in my head.

"What's a great idea?"

"This is what you're gonna do," I explain. "You're gonna hook-up with the next person that walks through the front door."

"What if she's-?"

"You can't be picky at a time like this. You need to move on, besides, that's what the beer is for."

John thinks about it for a minute, reaches deep for his sense of adventure and rips it from its hiding place. "Let's do it." He downs a full glass of beer and we stare at the bar entrance. The door opens and a big, fat, biker guy enters. He's bald and has a beard down to his waist.

John turns to me and gives me a look like, "Don't say it!"

"I bet the beard tickles." I couldn't help it.

John isn't laughing as we turn our attention back to the door and wait for the next *female* to enter.

Time passes slowly as nobody is coming in. John finishes another beer. I can tell his newly found sense of adventure is waning.

"This is stupid. What are the chances that a hot girl that just happens to be interested in me is gonna walk through that door?"

"Probably very poor," I admit.

But at that moment the door slowly opens. I grab John's arm in anticipation and . . .

In strolls Melissa.

John turns to me in disbelief.

"Son of a beach. You're on your own. I can't help you with this one." I grab my beer and head to the bar to hunt for babes.

***

The last time John saw her, he was asking her to marry him. As we know, that didn't go very well. She was the last thing on his mind as that door opened. He has no intention of speaking to her except he can't help himself. He still has feelings for Melissa and he's not sure they'll ever go away. But that's not why he's going to say hi. He's going to say hi because it would just be too awkward to ignore her all night. Besides, that's the right thing to do.

He approaches her and expects a simple,

casual greeting before they retreat to separate ends of the bar. Melissa, instead, smiles widely and thrusts her arms around him, squeezing him tight. The sudden embrace resurrects wonderful, old times. Feeling her body so close to his brings back so many great memories. There's one problem. "Please stop," he begs her.

"What's wrong?" She asks.

"I have three broken ribs."

"I had no idea, you poor thing."

The truth is, her body felt great, it's the emotions of the situation that got to him. This was the woman he wanted to spend the rest of his life with. Now she's back, and he has a weird feeling her return has something to do with him.

John buys a round, and they cozy up to the bar and reminisce.

A few hours go by and the bar crowd has thinned. They could talk for days about the good times but they're both buzzed and feeling a little antsy. Melissa suggests a game of bar shuffleboard. Despite John's lack of talent and Melissa's proclivity for bar sports, John agrees.

The game requires a smooth hand. John goes first, and awkwardly slides his blue disc, too rapidly. It ends up in the gutter. Melissa goes next and impressively slides her red disc onto the tip of the triangle at the end of the table for twenty points. She seductively blows on her fingertips like she's a nineteenth century gunslinger. John tries again and

171

slides his blue disc with far too much velocity. It slides off the edge into the gutter making a loud clunk.

"It's all about finesse," Melissa explains. She slides her second red disc, and it sits right next to her other one, scoring another twenty points.

John picks up his third blue disc and pauses.

"I know fire-fighters don't specialize in finesse. Let me help," Melissa says, taking advantage of the hesitation. She stands behind John, puts her left arm around his waist and her right hand on top of his right hand that holds the disc.

The tension mounts as her breasts press against his back prompting John to recall why he never learned the game. They enjoy the feel of each other's body. But the moment is interrupted by loud moans emanating from the back of the bar.

***

This is awesome. I'm tongue wrestling a red-head in a bar. Red-heads make up less than ten percent of the population. But what now? We're in a bar.

"Get a room," I hear Melissa shout from across the bar.

Great idea, I pull the red-head into the bathroom.

***

"That's not what I meant," Melissa says, regretfully.

"You should have been more specific," John says.

They get back to the game and Melissa guides John's hand as he pushes the disc. It slides to the other end of the table knocking both of Melissa's discs into the gutter and stopping perfectly on the triangle for twenty points.

John breaks the tension and takes undue credit, "I am the man; beat that."

Melissa smiles confidently accepting the challenge. She slides her last, red disc and knocks John's blue disc into the gutter. Her red disc is the last one standing, and she wins.

"Well played," John says with a terrible British accent.

Melissa laughs softly, looks around and says, "I never imagined I would miss this bar, but I did. I missed you too."

John thought his ears would rejoice at the sound of those words. He knows where she's going with this and the wonderful sound of an ex-girlfriend crawling back to him should make his night. But it doesn't. In fact, he's suddenly uncomfortable and silent.

"This would be a good time to tell me you missed me," Melissa says.

"Are you kidding? I thought about you all day, every day for six months. Half a year I dragged my butt from home to work and work to home. You were all I could think about. But then I met someone else."

"Can I ask who?"

"No," John bluntly replies.

Melissa turns her head, annoyed. She understands that she has no right to know but; "Is it Madison Park?"

173

"Since when do you read the tabloids?"

"Since my ex-boyfriend made the cover of 'Teen Beat' magazine."

"I made the cover?"

"Isn't she marrying Jorden Vandermear?"

"It's Vanderpool," John says correcting her. "I didn't say our relationship was perfect."

Melissa is upset. The atmosphere is very awkward. "I should go," she says.

John doesn't argue.

Melissa puts her drink on the bar and walks past John in a huff. Then she turns, goes back and gives him one last, strong hug. Then she leaves for good.

"Ouch," John says after the door closes behind her.

"Love hurts," the bartender strangely says.

"You have no idea," John says, holding his ribs.

John pulls up a barstool, when passionate yelps emanate from the bathroom. John thinks to himself, "I really do not need to hear my best friend's voice in the 'throws of passion'." The moans get louder until finally, they culminate in a toilet flushing. John and the bartender's befuddled looks say it all.

***

The firehouse has been quiet in the last couple of weeks. We had our hot streak, and now it's a little slow. It's good and bad. It's always good when homes aren't burning down, but unfortunately for John, it gives him a lot of time to think. As we play cards in the other room, he sits alone in the kitchen.

174

Frank enters the firehouse kitchen for a drink. He sees John looking pretty somber and asks, "How are the ribs healing?"

"They're feeling better every day," John says.

"So what is it then? Why so quiet? Wait, let me guess; the girl you're crazy about is marrying someone else tomorrow."

"What is it with her?" John says. "One minute she's declaring her love for me and the next minute, she's marrying Jorden Vanderpool. What happened?"

"Why don't you ask her?"

"She's getting married tomorrow," John says.

"So, if she's the one, go get her."

"You make it sound so easy," John says, frustrated.

"You run into burning buildings for a living, why be afraid of this?"

"What are you talking about?"

"You're afraid of what you may lose by being with her." Frank ventures, "You're worried that the price will be too high."

John realizes he's been exposed.

"So here's my humble advice," Frank says. "If there's one thing I can take away from twenty years of blissful marriage, it's this; the price is never too high."

Frank leaves John alone with his thoughts.

John sits in silence for a few minutes then says to himself, "So what am I supposed to do, jump on a plane and crash her wedding? That's crazy."

11

Not Your Typical Wedding Story

On the airplane the next morning John sits next to a young girl as they wait for takeoff. John has always been a pretty sensible guy but this is a matter of the heart so screw sensibility. John isn't even sure he's gonna make it in time but he figured he'd book the earliest flight and give it a shot. Precious time is already being lost as the flight attendant has just announced an hour delay due to traffic on the runway. Only at Laguardia Airport would there be traffic on the runway.

As John sits impatiently, the young girl in the seat next to him brazenly asks with a Midwestern accent, "Watcha' goin' to Oklahoma for?"

"I'm going to crash a wedding," John proudly responds. "You see, I'm in love with a girl who's marrying someone else."

"That's so romantic," the little girl gushes. "I hope that one day a tall, dark, handsome boy has the guts to rescue me just as I'm being forced to marry the evil prince."

John chuckles, thinking the little girl has seen way too many Disney movies.

"What's her name?" The girl asks.

"Madison," John says carefully.

"As in Madison Park?"

"You've heard of her?" John asks, knowing she has.

"Duh, who hasn't?" She says stubbornly. "She belongs with Jorden. They were made for each other. It's written in the stars. They're long time sweethearts. You really shouldn't talk about breaking them up like that." The little girl is upset now as she adds, "What's wrong with you? You're sick." She yells out for her mom as John slithers in his seat in a feeble attempt to hide.

***

I am so nervous. The preparations are in full swing as an army of service workers are in high gear. The ceremony is being held outdoors, here, on the Park Estate, under a perfect, autumn sky. The grounds are decorated the way only a millionaire, teen idol could afford to decorate. Just as she wanted, thousands of flowers, ice sculptures, a twenty-piece orchestra, caviar. You name it — if it's excessive and unnecessary, it's here.

At this point, nobody is as important as I am, though — because it is I who is at this very moment — sculpting the perfect wedding day hair. I won't lie, I think she's marrying the wrong man but I took care of everything. I poisoned the shrimp cocktail. I'm kidding, of course. I thought about it, but then I remembered

Jorden doesn't eat shellfish. So I poisoned all the other food. No I didn't, but I have to do something – but what? It's not easy pondering a diabolical scheme, while focusing on making Maddy exceptionally beautiful – as she makes the biggest mistake of her life. "I am so nervous," I tell her, as I work my magic with her hair. "I've looked forward to this day my whole life."

"It's my wedding," she reminds me.

"It's our wedding," I remind her. "Why am I more excited than you?" I think to myself, "Maybe it's because she's marrying the wrong guy."

"It kind of happened so fast," she says, opening up.

"Most people have what's known as 'an engagement'."

"You know me, when I want to do something, I just do it," she says.

"That kind of spontaneity is fine when you're buying a pair of shoes. You're only gonna wear 'em once anyway – if you know what I mean. We're talking about the rest of your life here."

"I know what we're talking about," she snaps.

I don't know where I got the big ones to ask her but I felt it needed to be asked and no one else was gonna do it. "Do you love Jorden?"

"It's more complicated than that," she says, after a long pause.

"Nothing's more complicated than love, sister."

"I have a career to think about," she sadly tries to explain. "Do you have any idea how many young, talented, motivated entertainers there are out there just waiting for me to fall? I'm on top, and I almost threw it all away for a silly, thrill-seeking boy."

"You sound like Angie."

"Maybe I should think more like Angie."

"Yeah, it's safer. If you actually lived your life your way you might get hurt, and we can't have that." Now I'm pissed and I feel the need to defend the fireman's honor, "By the way, John Kelly is no boy. He is more of a man than Jorden will ever be."

***

John desperately hails a cab at the Oklahoma National Airport. It's not quite like New York where they are lined up as far as the eye can see. He sees one but realizes another guy sees it too. They both run for the lone cab. Luckily the other guy is a businessman, and loafers are no match for Nike's. John gets in the cab and the other guy accepts defeat graciously – (which would never happen in New York). As soon as John catches his breath, he tells the cab driver to take him to the Park Estate.

"You've got to be kidding? The cabby says

laughing out loud. "I can't get within ten miles of that place."

"Get me as close as you can," John says.

***

The trees surrounding the grounds of the Park Estate explode with the magnificent colors of autumn. The season has meshed seamlessly and splendidly with the monumental affair.

Since Cynthia Santana and Hollywood Today received exclusive rights, the other paparazzi had to find other ways to get their story. That's why several helicopters hover overhead.

Guests mingle on the picturesque grounds as cocktail hour has already begun. The ceremony will take place afterward, with the reception following.

Outside the gates are hundreds of other media personnel who are unable to afford helicopters. Thousands of overenthusiastic fans join them.

***

Miles away, the city is abuzz as the cab comes to a stop.

"This is as close as you're gonna get. The estate is about ten miles south of here," the cabby says.

John gets out on a deserted corner in a strange city. Before the cab pulls away, the window goes down and the cabby shouts, "Good luck."

John looks around as if to formulate a plan. But

he's in an unfamiliar place where he knows nobody and he just doesn't have time to walk ten miles. His once-in-a-lifetime, spontaneous, romantic gesture is about to come to an abrupt and disappointing end. Then he sees something across the street – a firehouse.

***

Lights flash and sirens blare as John rides in the tiller seat of the fire truck. Unlike New York, the cars immediately yield for the fire truck as it coasts through the streets of the small city. In the front seat of the fire truck, an Oklahoma City firefighter drives and a lieutenant smokes a cigar in the passenger seat.

"This is the most fun I've had in years," the lieutenant proclaims.

Steering the back of the rig with one hand, John has his cell phone in the other. He pleads, "Come on, answer the phone, Madison." Suddenly he hears a voice pick up at the other end, "Hello."

***

When that iPhone went off and that sexy picture of John in his fireman gear, with black soot on his face and messy but sexy hair came up I jumped to answer it. "It's me, Quentin. What's all that noise?"

"It's a fire truck," John explains. "I'm on my way to the wedding right now."

"You better hurry up, the ceremony's about to start." My heart is gonna burst from my chest at the romance that's playing out right now.

181

"I need your help," he says.

***

The front gate is a surprisingly controlled mob scene. Thousands of fans are lined up just hoping to catch a glimpse of celebrity. In a small booth, two security guards sit and stare into the crowd when one asks, "Do you hear something?"

In the distance, the fire truck barrels toward the gate. The other security guard says, "It's a fire truck."

"I know that, dummy, but why? I don't see a fire anywhere," the guard says, as he peers at the twenty small, security, television monitors.

***

In the front cab of the fire truck, the driver says to the lieutenant, "The gates aren't opening."

"You noticed that too, huh," The lieutenant says. "The kid said he'd take care of it; full steam ahead."

***

The celebrity guests and family are all in their seats. A hush comes over the grounds as the orchestra plays "Here Comes the Bride." Angie walks Madison down the aisle, arm in arm.

Madison can't help but think this is one moment she wishes she could share with her father.

Cynthia and her cameraman film the ceremony.

Steven Stanton is one of the guests. He looks on anxiously. All he can think is, "Cha-ching."

***

Nervous is an understatement to describe the driver of the fire truck. He is rapidly approaching the closed gate. But the security guards refuse to open the gate with no direct evidence of a fire. Despite the impending disaster, the lieutenant seems strangely calm as he smokes his cigar. Suddenly, he sees a man running from the mansion, toward the security booth, thrashing his arms above his head screaming, "Fire, fire!"

***

That's me by the way. I can't believe I'm doing this. I have the greatest job in the world, and I could be throwing it all away. But this girl deserves better than a cheating, scheming, song-stealing, turtleneck-wearing in hot weather, little boy. She deserves a man. And to tell you the truth, it's quite liberating.

The security guards step from the booth to meet me and ask, "Where is the fire?"

I know that mansion better than anyone. When we were kids, Madison and I would play hide-and-go-seek. She could never find me. I tell them the only place that's not covered by security cameras, "The storage closet."

"There's no camera in the storage closet," one guard says to the other. That same guard reaches for

183

the lever to allow the speeding fire truck through.

But the other guard grabs his hand, stopping him and says, "Unless those firefighters each have an invitation they ain't getting through."

The fire truck closes in.

***

As the truck barrels toward the closed front gate, the driver gives the lieutenant a look, questioning his faith in John.

At the back of the truck John is anxious, as he mumbles to himself, "Don't let me down, Quentin."

The driver is seconds away from slamming into the front gate when, suddenly, the gates open. John rejoices in the tiller seat.

***

I can't believe he doubted me. As the truck barrels through the open gate John waves to me as I'm draped over the lever. The two guards eventually pry me from the lever and close the gate but it's too late. The fire truck is through along with about a thousand fans that dashed through behind it.

On the truck, John, again rejoices for a brief moment and then calms and asks himself, "Okay, now what?"

***

Jorden and Madison are completely unaware

of the events taking place at the front gate as they stand side by side in the presence of the minister, who asks that all important question, "If there is any person or persons here today that are against the union of Madison Park and Jorden Vanderpool, please speak now or forever hold your peace."

Suddenly, in the distance the faint sound of a fire truck's air horn is heard.

"What was that?" Madison perks up.

"I didn't hear anything," Jorden says. He turns to the minister and says, "Continue."

***

On the fire truck the lieutenant comes over the intercom, "John, what now?"

"According to Hollywood Today, the ceremony is being held in the back yard," John says over the intercom.

"I don't expect they're gonna let us walk through the house and a twenty foot wall surrounds the grounds," the lieutenant says. "They have more security than Fort Knox."

"I have an idea," John says.

***

I fend off the security guards and head back to the ceremony chasing the fire truck. I'm sprinting as fast as I can. I'm like Carl Lewis on Red Bull. We've been best friends our entire lives – Madison and me.

185

You think the girl would realize I'm missing at the biggest moment of her life. She's gonna hear it from me.

***

The minister smiles and says; "It is now time for Jorden and Madison to proclaim their love for each other through the sacrament of marriage. They have chosen traditional vows." The minister takes a moment as the crowd readies for them to profess their love for each other. Then he asks, "Do you Jorden Vanderpool, take Madison Park to be your lawfully wedded wife. To love, honor and obey, for richer, for poorer, in sickness and in health, till death do you part?"

"I do. Now, hurry up."

The minister turns to Madison, "Do you Madison Park, take Jorden to be your lawfully wedded husband? To love, honor and obey, for richer, for poorer, in sickness and in health, till death do you part?"

Madison subtly peers over her shoulder as if looking for advice from someone – anyone. Suddenly, she realizes she's making a big mistake. What has she gotten herself into? She hesitantly, turns back to the minister and stutters, "I, I-."

Suddenly, from above the wall surrounding the

186

ceremony the fire truck's bucket reaches out over the fence. John is inside the bucket. A hush comes over the crowd. Angie immediately gets on her walkie-talkie and summons additional security to the back yard.

***

At that very moment, I burst through the patio doors. The security guards follow, chasing me. In hindsight, I probably should have run in the opposite direction. But I can't miss this.

"That was fast," Angie says to herself. Then she yells to the guards, "Get him!"

Cynthia Santana's cameraman films the whole thing as she whispers to him, "I smell an Emmy."

John smoothly rappels from the bucket directly above Jorden, who gets out of the way.

The big bodyguard and security guards run toward John.

"Stop!" Madison shouts with a hand held high.

They stop.

I'll handle this," she calmly says.

John is center stage as everyone waits for an explanation.

***

Back at the firehouse, Captain Jack, Frank and I are preparing the meal in the kitchen. The television creates background noise. But we're focused on our

187

meal prep. I have a knife in one hand, and an onion in the other. A cutting board sits on the table in front of me and I feel the need to announce, "I hate chopping onions. They sting my eyes. It seems like we have onions with every meal."

"You think that's a coincidence, Billy?" Frank says.

"Oh my God," I respond – not to Frank but the television. "John is rappelling from the bucket on national T.V. That's totally against procedures."

"What?" Frank asks.

"Look." I point to the television. "Who gave him this idea?"

"I think I did," Frank says.

We're glued to the television as we wait for John to say what he has to say.

***

Suddenly the gravity of the situation hits John. Millions are watching and he freezes, momentarily. Even he can't believe what he's doing. Maybe he should have prepared something because, as the pressure builds, John slips into New Yorker mode when he says, "Are you kidding me with this charade? I can't believe you made me travel twelve hundred miles to bust this up."

"What?" Madison blurts out, shocked.

"If we're gonna have a future together, this

188

prima-donna stuff is not gonna fly," John says. "Every time things get a little difficult, you can't go off and marry your ex-boyfriend – on television."

"I'm her fiancé!" Jorden says.

John turns to him and, although the intense look in his eyes says it all, he asks, "Would you excuse us?"

What he means is, shut up and step aside.

Jorden does just that.

Madison looks John in the eyes and so desperately wants to leap into his arms. But she wasn't playing a game. She didn't do this so he could make a play for her. He's got it all wrong. With a tear in her eye, she explains, "I thought I lost you. I can't go through that again. I'm not strong enough to lose someone I love. Not again."

"I won't let anything happen to me," John assures her.

"You can't guarantee that."

"No, but I guarantee that I love you," he says, as he takes her hand. "And I guarantee that he doesn't. Isn't love worth it?"

Madison still waivers, as the thought of losing him like she lost her father seems to be too much to bear.

She's about to shock the world and turn away from John when, suddenly, Angie steps up and says, "Maddy, I was the happiest woman in the world raising chickens and living in a two bedroom ranch with your father. No amount of money or success will ever equal the love I had for that man. I would give every penny back for five more minutes with him. There is no substitute for true love. Don't let him go."

Madison looks at John with tears in her eyes.

John, slightly embarrassed, says, "I get that same funny feeling in my gut when I'm with you."

Struggling to keep from breaking down Madison says through her tears, "Are you saying I make you sick?"

"Something like that," John says with a smile, as he feels he's convinced her.

As the tears roll down her cheeks, Madison smiles big and leaps into John's arms. He squeezes her tight as the crowd applauds.

***

Back at the firehouse, we all applaud as John kisses Madison on the television screen.

I can't help but cry like a baby as these freakin' onions are burning the crap out of my eyes.

***

John and Madison are still locked in a strong

embrace. As John scans the grounds, he says to Madison, "I was going to bring you roses but you never mentioned the other fifty dozen I sent to your hotel room back in New York."

"That was you," Madison says. She gives Jorden a look that makes him cringe and hide behind the big bodyguard.

To further disrupt the wonderful moment, Steven Stanton jumps in and scolds Jorden, "Don't you have any pride; any guts? Are you going to stand there and let him steal your woman?"

Jorden comes out of hiding behind the big bodyguard and comes clean. "If anyone was trying to steal a woman it was me. I've been a jerk." He turns to Madison. "Your feelings for John were obvious the minute I arrived in New York. Watching you in the hotel room behind the flowers, I could tell you really cared about him. I shouldn't have gotten in the way of that. I hope you can forgive me."

Madison gives him a small friendly hug in forgiveness.

Jorden then turns to Steven and says, "You're fired."

"You can't fire me," Steven arrogantly insists.

"I just did," Jorden says.

Madison asks the security guards to remove Steven.

As he's physically escorted out he yells, "You're finished; washed up. You'll never have another record again – ever. You haven't heard the last of me."

With Steven gone, Jorden cups his ear, hears nothing, and says, "Actually we just did." Jorden then reaches his hand out to John in forgiveness. John, happily, grips it tight and they shake.

Madison turns to Jorden, "How would you like to open up for me on my concert tour?"

"Me, 'an opening act' for the great Madison Park? I would be honored."

Madison turns back to Angie and says, "Thanks mom." It was the first time she had referred to her as mom since her dad died. She turns back to John and gives him another big kiss and the crowd cheers.

I haven't cried like this since they canceled "Sex And The City." Although, there was that time I got my eyebrows waxed.

***

You might think the guests were disappointed but it was quite the opposite. They got a better show than anyone expected. In fact, Cynthia Santana did win an Emmy and is now an anchorwoman for Hollywood

Today. The party went on late through the night and into the wee hours of the morning.

Not wanting it to end, John and Madison sit alone in a distant gazebo, surrounded by reddish-orange roses, enjoying a beautiful, autumn sunrise.

The end

About the author:

Terry Brody is a New York City fire lieutenant working in Queens. He has written several screenplays. Rescuing Madison is his first book, and is based on the screenplay of the same name. He wrote the produced short film, "Beer, Chocolate or You" which can be seen on the website: www.minimovie.com. He is currently adapting his award winning horror/thriller screenplay "Adrian of Death" to a book.   More information can be obtained on www.IMDB.com.